PAINT THE BIRD

GEORGEANN PACKARD

THE PERMANENT PRESS • SAG HARBOR, NEW YORK

Library of Congress Cataloging-in-Publication Data
Packard, Georgeann.
    Paint the Bird / Georgeann Packard.
    pages cm
    ISBN 978-1-57962-317-3
    1. Religious life—Fiction.   2. Life change events—Fiction.
    3. Artists—Fiction.   I. Title.
    PS3616.A329P35   2013

For further information, contact:

THE PERMANENT PRESS
4170 Noyac Road
Sag Harbor, New York 11963
www.thepermanentpress.com

For Bruno, Gunley, Cousy, Danny, Pahbie, and Ralphie

Siblings by chance, friends by choice

TO KEEP FAITH

TO HOLD FAST TO ILLUSORY THINGS

TO CHASE AN ILL-DEFINED AND EVASIVE LOVE

TO ATTEMPT TO RENDER THESE

IN COLOR, SHAPE, A PRETEND REALITY

IS TO PAINT THE BIRD

THE ONE IN FLIGHT

FLUID, ENSOULED, RAPTUROUSLY FORMLESS,

CONFINED BY MEMORY

IMPOSSIBLE TO PAINT

RARA AVIS, FAITH

CHAPTER ONE • RAW SIENNA

The Second Day After Ash Wednesday

I've read that a writer writes to understand what he is thinking.
A painter, one like me, paints to unearth what he is feeling...
then must find a way to bury again the pain he exhumes.

Abraham Darby

A WOMAN AND TWO MEN, ALL WITHOUT COATS, ARE SMOKING just outside the restaurant. Sarah has walked west along Christopher Street, then north on Washington, and comes to stand next to the three. They are now four corners of a square, the four directions on a map. Sarah is South.

The three strangers look at her, but Sarah stares at the door of Malatesta and the animated crowd beyond, though the entrance and her line of vision are partially blocked by East, the woman.

Sarah waits for clear passage but says nothing. The two men exhale in unison.

"Care for a smoke?" East asks.

Sarah does not smoke. "Yes, please. That would be lovely."

The woman pulls a hard pack from her massive purse, a thing that to Sarah resembles a cow's stomach.

The new cigarette is lit by the handsome, artsy, possibly gay West. They enjoy their cigarettes in silence. A couple enters the restaurant during this time, cupping their hands over mouths to protect them from the deadly fumes. They scurry in, seating is limited, no reservations. It's Friday night in the early stages of February.

The nicotine agitates Sarah and the past few weeks begin to eat at her. Today's questions had been kindly and respectfully put, insipid to the point of insult. She had no answers for them. The one thing she should have revealed, she would not. So on and on the all-male, clerical triumvirate skillfully prodded. Over and over, she told them that she herself did not understand. Her words, her actions, were as foreign to her as they surely must have seemed to them. The entire afternoon had resembled a block of slowly melting ice, yielding nothing more than a vacant pulpit to accompany her empty bed.

Now her companions' smoking is finished and Sarah realizes that they are waiting for her to snuff out her cigarette. An unwritten code perhaps. "I apologize for my distraction. Thank you." She regrets the formal tone of her words. They are inappropriate here.

"No worries," pipes North, and they all file into Malatesta. The others return to their table, the last of their wine, a small dish of custard and three forks. Sarah weaves her way to the bar at the far end of the small, crowded room. She removes her coat, folds it loosely, and places it atop the last stool available. Most backs are turned to her and arms flail in dangerously exaggerated gestures, but she takes possession of her circle of space on the stool.

There seems to be a problem in the kitchen, just to the right of the bar. Much commotion. Vocal eruptions in Italian. Unfortunately, the bartender gets pulled into it, deserting her in her time of need. He returns a few minutes later and finishes the opening and pouring of wine at the opposite end.

It's odd, she thinks, that in the everyday world she used to inhabit, she was treated almost as divine royalty, as though she could part waters to save the afflicted. She is someone many knew, although her first name is rarely uttered. But here she is simply black, older, overdressed. And that is fine.

Wine from a Mason jar spills to her immediate right, staining a white linen napkin a blackish red. A man turns to her, is sorry. "No worries," she repeats as she watches him dab the blotch.

Finally, the bartender, sweet and open-faced, is before her. "Forgive me. What can I get for you?" So many apologies, Sarah thinks, for so early in the evening.

"Martini. Gin, of course. Very dry. Extra olive." That kind of day.

On delivery, she finds the murky liquid instantly soothing, as comforting as a walk through a piney wood in autumn. She strolls through the first and orders another. The kitchen noise has dissipated or perhaps the noise in the room has folded voice into clatter, creating a cacophony of pleasant, mindless scraps of sound. All the tables are filled and more people huddle by the entrance waiting.

Sarah sees herself in the large antique mirror behind the bar and raises her glass in a toast. She feels as if she's in a Christmas ornament, amidst all the sparkling green bottles lining the shelves and the sentimental warm lighting that falls on the scene. She stares at the tall, commanding image of herself seated at the bar, the short-cropped, dense hair and the sturdy, still-sensuous torso. She could be a painting hanging there, an exotic Moroccan woman in an ordinary Italian bistro. Yes, she has the skin of an older woman, soft and worn, but the lines in her face are delicate, like skate tracks over fresh ice. How she has reached this age is a blurry mystery. She looks away.

The gin is eating away at the imagined walls that separate her from her comrades at Malatesta. She glances at the oversized clock rimmed in a worn, black-painted frame on the east wall. It reads what it always reads, 4:00.

There is a great warmth to this place—she has felt it whether here alone, or with her husband and, of course, most often with that apostate, the traitorous Bennetta. Sarah winces and vows to reclaim as her own the delicate light that spills from the paper shades on the tabletop lamps and the black-and-white, hexagonal ceramic tile on the floor, and is comforted further by the places where tiles are missing. *Can there possibly be beauty in loss?*

More people gather around the bar now, drinking while they wait for tables to clear. They are not unfriendly to her. There is a nod and smile from time to time, but they are wrapped tightly in their little circles of friends and lovers. And that is also fine as Sarah is quite cozy in her anonymity as she scans the room at will through the breaks between bodies.

Scattered randomly about are mismatched chairs and wooden tables of varying sizes and styles. Center stage is a massive table cut around a rustic structural post. Sarah's eyes keep coming back to it and its theatrical cast of diners—an older man and three others half his age. Licks of conversation are batted about the table. They seem to her not to know each other well but more likely share a common bond, as if they all owned Harleys or early Picassos or cafes. Who can say, but in her ginny staring, it is that older man who captures her attention. He's tall and solid, not so much heavy as dense. His gestures are equally grand, his hands flying about like wildly orbiting planets when he speaks.

Sarah turns on her stool and faces her own reflection once again. There she is with those oversized almond-shaped eyes and eyebrows that taper in an inquisitive upward swing. She watches herself raise her glass, take a slow sip, then smile seductively as if to a lover.

She had better eat something soon.

But she is too distracted to eat. Her eyes return to center stage and through the cover of others, she sees his white mane falling past his collar and pushed back in a dramatic sweep from the great expanse of his forehead. He seems not so much a man as a landscape with those cascading rivers of hair, broad plains of face and torso, peninsular appendages of arms and legs sprawling in all directions.

She indulges further. More striking than the blue black mussel shells in the glass bowl before him or the glittering green of the wine bottles, even more suggestive than the blood red stains on the tablecloth or the opulence of the golden candlelight that spills everywhere is the color of his eyes. Even from the bar, half the room away, the eyes seem lit from behind, mesmerizing, unworldly, the cold, clear blue of lake ice.

Sarah swirls back on her stool causing her white coat to fall to the floor. Everything she carries is stuffed into pockets as she never uses a purse, just one more thing to watch and guard, to weigh her down. She takes the long, heavy coat and hangs it on an already loaded coatrack nearby. One must cultivate trust.

Settling back on her stool she returns to her martini. Sarah straightens her dress, her frame of mind. She sips again and rests the glass on the worn oak of the bar. She hears laughter behind her and glances over her shoulder to see the three younger men with open mouths and heads back, one arm rests on another's shoulder and the bond does seem to her familial. But the man with the ice-colored eyes is motionless, looking past them, at nothing, or perhaps a memory. There is a sadness in this nervous hilarity. She's seen it at funerals. Then yet another bottle of wine is delivered to them by a swarthy, unshaven waiter. Smiling, ever nonjudgmental, he removes the cork, lifts and fills each glass, moves on.

Sarah hears the jazz fragments that punctuate the room chatter, reminding her of the echoes of organ notes and preservice chitchat. She redirects to simply watch the dance of all the lovely young men in black t-shirts and tight, faded blue jeans as they serve the Malatestans, dipping low with plates of gnocchi, clams, and over there, a heaping serving of spaghetti alla chitarra. She feels the gin coursing through her blood now, birthing a pleasant fog in her head.

Life in the moment, she observes privately, is her mantra now. Right now, here at Malatesta among strangers, the gift of a clear and magical moment. Surely worth a brief prayer of gratitude, were she able to pray.

Shifting from soul to stomach, Sarah picks up a menu, handwritten on butcher block paper. Cozze? No. Vongole? Maybe. Wait, better the grilled calamari. "And please the salad with the shaved cheese and some crusty bread. That would be perfect. Thank you." The bartender smiles sweetly and takes her wishes to the bright and noisy kitchen. It is still 4:00.

Quickly, the food arrives, accompanied by a small candle and a glass of wine of the deepest red.

"Thank you for the ambiance," Sarah says, "but I did not order wine." Her martini is not yet finished.

"This is his favorite Chianti. It seems you have an admirer." An annoying but somehow charming smirk splashes over the bartender's face.

"And who would that be?" she asks.

"Enjoy your dinner." The bartender takes away the last sip of the martini and then is off to other mischief.

Well, of course. She's been sitting there at the bar, analyzing this man's appearance, dissecting his relationships, staring like a schoolgirl. Bartenders miss little, being sober witnesses to the peculiarities of human nature. She turns on her stool and sees him in heated conversation with one of the other men. Now a shock of his white hair hangs in his eyes. His hand rests on another's shoulder and this advance seems to her unwelcome. She feels for the first time intrusive and returns to the still life objects before her, the flawless presentation of calamari, bread, and salad in the glowing medieval light. From habit, she turns to the clock, as if time could cure her unease, as if it were anything but 4:00.

Sarah touches the wine to her lips without sipping. She senses the grape, the fermentation over time, the luscious wood that held it. Then she takes a small sip and coats her mouth before swallowing. A small slice of the grilled calamari, silken, tender, smokey. Then the salty, nutty cheese. Swish of wine. Sacramental, earthy bread. Repeat.

She feels him there before seeing him. Smells the wool of his sweater, infused with winter air. She slowly chews what is in her mouth. Another sip of wine. Sees first his hand splattered with age spots and paint, the way he wears his watch with the face on the inside of his wrist.

"Abraham," he says, the *m* pulled like a final pluck on a bass fiddle.

"Sarah," she replies and smiles. "I believe we've met."

"I would remember."

"Genesis. We were in our nineties. The God of the Old Testament gave us a child at that age. Isaac…whom you later prepared for sacrifice."

"Sacrifice my own son?"

"On an altar of fire."

He frowns.

"An angel kept you from lighting the fire," she comforts him.

"My faith was that strong?"

"Yes."

He is quiet for a moment, lowers his head. She boldly touches his hair, brushes the wild shock from his eyes as his face comes to hers, uncomfortably close.

"But I am Abraham Darby. A different man."

"Yes, I see that. There is a rose with that name, you know."

He lifts her glass with a questioning look.

"Please," she says.

He kills the remainder. "I'm a little drunk. Sorry."

"Not so sober myself." She examines the two of them together in the mirror. "I've interrupted your dinner party."

"No. They've all left." He drags a stool near her and sits. She swears she hears the wood groan.

"Thank you for the wine, Abraham. It was so…unusually complex…and delicious."

"Well put. Call me Darby." He picks with his fingers from the greenery in her salad. Then a slice of the calamari. She finds this rude, but only a childlike rudeness.

Sarah hails the bartender. "May I have my bill, please?"

"The gentleman has paid both bill and gratuity." Again the smirk.

"I find that presumptuous. And very old school," she says to Darby.

He pops the last chunk of bread into his mouth. His face is so close now she is forced to look into his eyes, the lake ice blue now with a melted, watery coat.

"Could I be old school in a new way? A not presumptuous, just kinda nice guy way?" Here he burps but in a closed-mouth fashion that nearly knocks him off his stool.

Sarah turns from him but is smiling.

"Take a walk with me?" he asks shyly.

He retrieves her coat from the coatrack as though he had placed it there. She stares at him, but when he holds it open for her, she pulls it on, checks her pockets, buttons up. As he returns to his table to get his scarf and cap, Sarah takes in his size. She is five-nine and he is a head taller, of full frame but erect posture, even though intoxicated. He wraps his striped, schoolboy scarf twice around his thick neck and pulls on his black cabby's cap. No coat.

There he stands looking at her. Sarah puts her hands in her pockets and slowly walks towards him, dodging waiters, jutting chairs, the distracting noise, and pockets of light.

"You are a beautiful sight," he slurs once she reaches him. "Like a black angel."

She laughs. "The angel who keeps you from lighting the sacrificial fire?"

"Too late for that."

CHAPTER TWO • VENETIAN RED

The Third Day After Ash Wednesday

THEY TRAVEL AS ONE. HER PURE WHITE WOOLEN COAT AND his rumpled gray fisherman's sweater are woven into a new garment, one fashioned from listlessness and carnal needs. For both of them, whatever forgetting needed to be done, alcohol alone had not sufficed.

Darby and Sarah walk south on empty Washington Street just past midnight. The moist Hudson River air applies a layer of youth to their faces, the coolness in it energizing. Then onto Hubert Street where still there are few souls until they reach Hudson Street. There, people are smoking outside bars or hailing cabs or walking in twos, cuddled against the cold.

Sarah is a stranger to these streets and follows Darby through what she assumes is his neighborhood. One quick westward jag onto North Moore, a lick of West Broadway, and then they arrive at White Street, where unassuming Church Street morphs into the more ambitious Avenue of the Americas.

"This is home," Darby announces, gesturing to a black-painted column and three metal steps that mark the entrance to the six-story building. To the immediate left, she sees an upscale furniture store, loosely filled with cold, modern, angular furniture. At right is a more comforting gallery of rugs, hung like paintings, some resembling ancient tapestries and others multi-textured stripes of color.

While his hands search through pockets, he turns his large Minotaur head to her. "Would you like some tea or another glass of wine?"

There will be no tea. "Alright," Sarah hears herself say.

He takes the single key he has discovered, unlocks the door, and leads her into the small lobby, painted a harsh, bluish white and illuminated by a fluorescent bulb above. Mailboxes are lined up neatly at the left, and to the right, an elevator from another era. Accustomed to her former life of doormen and uptown marble lobbies resplendent with fresh flowers, she asks, "Is this thing safe?"

Darby yanks the metal gate open and then closes it behind them. "As safe as going home with a complete stranger." He smiles and plants a paternal kiss on the top of her head.

She is apprehensive but does not show it. When one gets to be of a certain age, risk-taking is as easy as it was fifty years prior. Immediate gain trumps loss in retrospect. His vague but desperate need tugs at her. It is her profession to empathize, to ease pain. But she knows her acquiescence has nothing to do with him.

They ascend to the top floor and a small hallway. One last metal door is unlocked and they are in his loft. In the vast open space she sees the articles of life that define his work, his habits, perhaps his state of mind. The floors are a paint-splattered wood plank, and in the center of the room is a long, simple table with the only current source of light, a lamp with a base shaped as a curling mermaid. There is also a wine bottle, one stout glass, take-out containers, loose papers. Two chairs accompany the table with a worn oriental rug beneath it all. She sees a small galley kitchen, and on the far wall, an unmade bed with a trio of lovely windows above and two circular windows high and off to each side. It gives the loft the solemnity and elegance of a French cathedral.

Sarah removes her coat, lays it on the back of a chair, and walks around the space. On the remaining walls lean canvases of various sizes, mostly large rectangles. Many face her and some are in vertical storage racks. A long, heavy table holds many messy tubes of paint, makeshift palettes, tins, jars of brushes, soiled cloths, a tidy stack of photographs, a loose pile of menus.

Abraham Darby scurries about the loft, tidying the bed, fluffing pillows, removing the take-out debris from the table, then pouring two shallow glasses of red wine.

Sarah comes again to the center of the loft, stands near the table. "Don't just fuss about," she tells him. "Sit with me." He does sit, swirls the wine in his glass, but does not drink.

"Darby, don't you want to know anything about me before we go to bed? I mean, that *is* what you have in mind."

"Yes. I mean, no. I have no questions for you. I see what I need to know."

"Are you curious about my marital status?"

"Not really. But as you see, I live alone. I should ask, I guess, if anyone is expecting you."

"Only you." Sarah removes her tall boots, her long skirt, then her stockings. She walks around the table. "I am 69 years old. Soon to be 70. When I remove the rest of my clothing, this is the woman you will see."

"Please, Sarah. Undress for me. I'm at the same age, a little older even. All grown up. I want to see all of you. Every curve. Every refinement of age."

Refinement of age? Sarah smiles. This is how an artist would define the effects of time and gravity. She looks around the loft, wishes she could see the paintings better, to know him a little more. Her eyes return to him and he has not moved.

"Alright, Darby. You look healthy enough for sexual activity." She pulls her pink sweater over her head, unbuttons and removes her blouse. She stands before him in the lamp's gentle, forgiving light clad only in her bra and underpants. Darby scrapes his chair nearer and brings his hands behind her, cups her buttocks and pulls her even closer towards him. He then unlatches Sarah's bra and slides her underpants down and off as she lifts each foot for him.

He stands and touches her eyelids, her hair, her full breasts beneath the dangling bra, then caresses the soft mound of her belly and between her legs. Sarah kisses him hard, opening his mouth with her tongue. She likes her nakedness against his clothed body, even the roughness of his sweater. Her hands are in his glorious hair, fine like corn silk. Perhaps he lifted her then or maybe they became some version of Chagall's flying lovers, but they are soon in his bed. They both work to undress him; there are many layers and his form is not conducive to this horizontal striptease. But soon enough and after some laughter they are exploring each other's bodies as the city continues with its business of tiring out its most hardy inhabitants. Here in the loft no traffic noises or arguments or footsteps or any of the symphonic chords of city life can be heard. There is only the moaning and panting of these two mature lovers, youthfully amateurish in Darby's oversized bed.

As Darby is stroking slowly inside her, he whispers into her ear, "What is your favorite color?"

"What?"

"Your favorite color?"

"Purple," she manages.

"Your favorite city?"

"Amsterdam," she exhales.

"The book that influenced you the most?"

Sarah is tiring of this game but can't stop him. "Darby," she moans. "The Bible?"

"Painting?" He quickens his strokes.

"I love Tamayo."

She so craves to be only in her body at this moment, but asks him, "What music do you...listen to..." and she slows his thrusts "...when you're down?"

"Coltrane. You?"

"Nina Simone," she says without thinking.

She is near orgasm, frantic for it, her palms on her temples. Her body moves with his, then she stiffens and clamps her fingers around the top of the headboard. But then he stops completely and only the movement of his breathing slips her into a shaking, near epileptic orgasm as he lies still within her.

When Sarah opens her eyes, Abraham Darby is magically on his back beside her. *How did he get there?* She feels cold and exposed in the ambient light of the city and distant table lamp. She can see, however, the crowd of portraits against the wall nearest the bed, subtle accusations delivered in violent greens and a shroud of judgment in the deepest purples. She sits up and looks at Darby. His eyes are closed and he is breathing softly. His hair flows gently away from his face onto the pale blue pillowcase like wisps of cloud in a summer sky. It seems that whatever he was looking for in this chance coupling, he has found. But on closer examination she discovers tension in his jaw, his hands, the curl of his toes. There is much more to lose.

She examines her own body, expecting to see a younger woman's form but it is as it has grown to be, deeper in hue, less toned, every part laden with the weight of so many years. But still...there is life in it, and yes, the ability to seduce and please a man. She takes this body and lays it over Darby's. He sighs. The strangeness of it all dissipates and it is simply now again the 19th of February. Three days ago it was Ash Wednesday.

Darby pulls a blanket over them and then another. "Sleep here with me, Sarah. I have to ask you something...to do for me...tomorrow."

As if she has no plans, no obligations for Saturday. No weekend domestic chores or socializing with family or friends. No visits to the sick, baptisms, or burial site prayers. But, as it happens, she has none of these.

"My day is free," is all she says. Soon she too is easing into sleep, while the artist's fingers sketch small abstractions across her back.

A few hours later, they have separated and he rises and goes to the center table. With pencil on paper he writes for some thirty minutes, then takes out his favorite corduroy jacket, black slacks, a decent shirt, even a tie. And the black dress. He hangs these things on the outside of his clothes cupboard. Clears the table. Turns out the light. Then holds on to Sarah for dear life.

‡ ‡ ‡

Sarah wakes when she always wakes, just before six. She had not slept well. Darby was like a human furnace and she kept rolling away from him, only to find him soon reattached. The refrigerator roared inefficiently and there was a loud buzzing that might actually have been *inside* her head. She now has an impressive hangover, her mouth void of saliva and her head pulsing with pain.

She molts the draping Darby and stands naked in the weak light. A full-length mirror is propped against a near wall and she walks to it. Sarah examines the woman before her, not critically but as if the two had just met. What sin has this woman just indulged in with a man she does not know? What penance appropriate for loving his boyish eagerness, his silly questions and the way he stayed motionless inside her? She finds she doesn't care.

This is sex, she concludes. But is it always better with strangers?

Outside of marriage? She thinks of William and their withered sex life. And hadn't she confided in Bennetta that she quite preferred it that way? Sarah turns away from the woman in the mirror.

The loft is cool, so she wraps his heavy shirt around her and searches for the bathroom. It is a tiny room with a door that does not fully close. She drinks long directly from the faucet and then sits on the toilet, one hand clutching the cold curve of the claw-foot tub just to her left. It is a man's bathroom, but surprisingly clean, and not unlike her own in its simplicity. She washes her face, brushes her teeth with his toothbrush—so unlike her to do that. She opens the medicine chest, and amidst the Old Spice, the first aid supplies, and the pain relievers, she finds a product called Corn Huskers Lotion. It is gelatinous, odorless, and odd. Sarah rubs it into her face and hands. Swallows two aspirins.

A feathery light drifts into the loft space and she can better discern the crowd of paintings that hang high on walls and lean against them. It is a gallery of faces and bodies, buried in a thick application of paint, but also vividly representational in style. The intensity of color explodes in the soft light—whites rich in blues and purples, blues laced with sensual greens. There are nudes and ancient faces; a young girl on a subway, many portraits of a boy, another boy who might be the same boy but older. Many paintings of a seductive young man are grouped together with random, empty spaces where paintings may have been removed. There are sketches in stacks and even murals of figures painted on the white walls.

She goes to the kitchen and turns on a small radio, replacing the jazzy static with her own classical station. There must be some piece of her in this unfamiliar landscape. She finds coffee, a French press, cream still in its prime. Sarah toasts some fresh-enough sourdough bread she finds in the fridge. There is butter and a jam crystallized with age.

Darby rises, grabs his robe, takes his suit and a few things from an oak bureau, and disappears into the bathroom. As Sarah pours the hot water into the press, she hears him washing, brushing his teeth. He emerges as she pours two mugs of coffee.

"Good morning, Sarah," he says formally.

She looks at him standing before her in his jacket and crumpled dress shirt. The jacket is open and she sees that the back end of his tie is longer than the front. She removes it from his neck, puts it around her own, and reties it properly.

"How are you, Mr. Darby? What is it that I can do for you today?" She would prefer climbing back into his bed with him, but doubts that is his intent.

He walks to the cupboard and returns with the black dress on its hanger. It is a heavy, form-fitting affair with a scoop neck, long sleeves.

"I imagine this will fit you. Please put it on and come with me to Brooklyn."

"Where in Brooklyn?" she asks, gawking at the dress that looks much too small for her.

"If I tell you, you might not come, but it would mean a lot to me if you did. I need you."

"You don't know me well enough to need me," she says. "You need someone."

CHAPTER THREE • IVORY BLACK

WHITE STREET IS AWASH IN FEBRUARY'S TENTATIVE NATURE, caught between the worst of winter and hope for spring. The temperature hangs right around freezing but the wind is sharp. The day is sunny but aggressive clouds lounge in the western sky. Very quickly they are back on Canal Street.

"Let's take the A," Darby says. "We can grab the F at Jay Street."

"And our final destination is?" Sarah asks.

"Carroll Gardens. In Brooklyn."

As they work their way through the crowded street, Sarah sees a man in a large black coat stoop to drop some change into the upturned hat of another man sitting on the sidewalk, wrapped in blankets. The upright man tears away half of the bagel he's eating and hands it to the apparently homeless man. Both then hold their bagels briefly aloft, a toast. "To better times!" she hears the seated man exclaim as she passes.

A street vendor greets Darby by name and smiles at her. Darby picks through the hats, scarves, and gloves on his cart and selects a bright orange and red plaid scarf that feels like—but is not made of—the downy wool of a Kashmir goat.

"How much for this, Eddie?" Darby asks, holding it up next to

Sarah's face. She notices many caps just like Darby's in a neat stack and wonders if much of his wardrobe is picked up on the street. The vendor, a couple shades darker than Sarah, has the exact scarf wrapped around his neck and tucked into his faux leather jacket.

"For my lovely sister, only ten dollars," he says.

"I'll give you ten, but only if you stop flirting with my date."

"You drive a hard bargain, Abe, my brother. But you got a deal. And I'll keep my eyes to home."

Darby wraps the scarf around Sarah's neck in a way she never would, with both ends thrown behind her, as if she were going ice skating.

"Nice to see you dating within your age group, Abe, if not within your people," the vendor shouts after him.

"Shut up, Eddie. She's way younger than me."

Almost to Thompson, a shop sprawls onto the sidewalk. The sign above boasts *Electronics* but there is little of that. More prevalent than the powerstrips, outlets, and hairdryers are broken African masks, chipped marble elephants, and boxes filled with tiny baby shirts that read, "If I don't sleep, nobody sleeps." Sarah rewraps her scarf and they descend into mass transit.

When they board the train, they are greeted by an actual woman's voice, not the common digital one. "Step all the way in," as opposed to clogging the doorways. "This is the A to Far Rock." The car is not crowded and they easily find two seats together. The gentle jerking and swaying of the train as they begin their journey to Brooklyn is pleasant for Sarah; she rarely rides the subway and so enjoys the kaleidoscope of humanity around her. Here the plain white folks are the minority; dominant are Chinese, Latino, Indian, African American, blends of those, and many more. There's a woman hunched over needlepoint, another reading *Good Housekeeping*. Many are attached by wires to their life-support devices, their personal libraries of music or information, or play with their phones. It is surprisingly quiet. Sarah marvels at the collection of outstanding headgear, from smart leather derbies to earmuffs, scarves, and every manner of baseball cap, all cocked in self-identifying positions on their owners' heads. One woman appears to be wearing her pajamas under her puffy nylon jacket.

When the doors open at Chambers Street, there stands but one person, as though the curtains on a stage had parted for a single actress. Sarah examines the young woman of not even 20 years, really just a girl, lacking any sophistication or trappings of adulthood. She hesitates and does not board, but just as the doors begin to close, she dodges into the car with a blurred quickness.

She takes the seat directly across from Sarah. Her wild eyes are an unnatural green and her black hair is chopped, uncombed. She wears a bandanna that is tied behind her at the nape of her neck, with symbols that look like cave drawings imprinted on the cloth. Her coat is made of some kind of animal skin and her jeans are torn. It is her footwear that may be the oddest part of the ensemble, looking like the crusty, shaggy feet of what, Sarah can't say, perhaps a llama or a mountain goat. She has an old-fashioned satchel that she now sorts through, pulling out books, cigarettes, an apple, a small wooden flute. Could she be a student, Sarah wonders. *But of what?* She already has an aura of self-knowledge and experience beyond her tender years.

The girl looks up, meets Sarah's staring eyes, and glares back, defiant and challenging. Her deep golden skin takes on the greenish, unnatural light of the subway car and Sarah is uncomfortable, but doesn't look away. They remain like this for some time, as the car rocks along the tracks. Stops are announced, doors open and close, people pass between them. It's as though they are having some deep, wordless conversation, sharing the stories of their lives through their locked eyes.

Sarah's heart is pounding erratically, and breaking a bit, too, at the sight of this waif's vast vulnerability and yet deeper strength. She feels the need to protect her, but knows she herself may be the weaker one. Darby seems engrossed in the study of the blank space before him, so she excuses herself from his company and crosses the car to sit next to the girl.

"Hello," Sarah says, like a question.

"Hi," she answers in a child's apprehensive voice.

"I'm intrigued by your...look...and your face. May I ask...your heritage is?"

"Mexico. Lakota. Mars."

"I see. My people came from western Africa. Later, Chicago."

"I think you're very beautiful," the girl says. "I like your long nose and the color of your skin. May I touch your hair?"

"Yes, of course." And the child-woman takes her open palm and lays it on Sarah's head, gently at first and then adding weight.

"Are you blessing me?"

"If you'd like me to."

"Yes," Sarah answers, a little unsure. Then, "Yes. I would."

The girl removes her hand, gets up solemnly, and stands directly in front of her mature counterpart. She floats both hands, open like wings with thumbs nearly touching, just above Sarah's scalp. She closes her eyes and whispers with a chant-like rhythm. Sarah can't decipher the words at all, but she closes her eyes and breathes in all the scents that cling to the girl. It's an intoxicating mix of damp moss, pinesap, vanilla, and a candle just after it's blown out, and then a lingering finish of tingling fresh salt air. So sensually charged is Sarah that she can almost hear the rushing waters of the East River as they pass through the tunnel to the next borough.

When Sarah opens her eyes, the doors are closing at High Street in Brooklyn and the girl is miraculously gone. In her lap, she finds a battered holy card of Christ in the garden, his pleading eyes heavenward. As she returns to her seat, the train lurches and she is nearly tossed into the lap of Abraham Darby.

"Stranger things have happened," he tells her. "Once I was sitting across from two young lovers. Their arms and legs were all knotted together and they whispered and kissed as the F train rambled on. The young man stood, gathered his gear, and exited at this very stop in Brooklyn. The love and sorrow expressed at their parting was akin to a new husband returning to war.

"It was just a silly, adolescent romance, but I felt her very real pain as she sat there without him, unwhole, clutching her backpack against her chest with one hand, the other hand flat against the warmth of his seat."

"Sweet, Darby, but not strange," Sarah comments.

"That's not the weird part. She caught me looking at her and in her face I could see that she was pitying *me!* She probably saw this bulky, disheveled old man who possessed no love as great as hers. Then she smiled so sweetly at me and strapped on her backpack, walked directly over to me, and kissed me right on the mouth. I mean a real kiss, not a little peck. Then she swirled around and hopped off the train at Smith Street. Doors closed. My stop was the next one, but I didn't get off. Rode the train all the way out to Coney Island and all the way back to Carroll Street."

Sarah looks around the subway car. No one is speaking at the moment; everyone seems lost in his or her own world, reading newspapers and novels, still attached to devices, sleeping. The woman doing needlepoint puts it into a large canvas bag, buttons her coat.

"Next stop is ours," Darby announces. "Was that kid blessing you?"

"She tried, but it was like blessing a stone." Sarah jams the holy card into her pocket and adds, almost bitterly, "Take me to wherever it is you need me to be."

CHAPTER FOUR • DIOXAZINE PURPLE

THEY WALK IN THE CARROLL GARDENS NEIGHBORHOOD OF Brooklyn, down Carroll Street to the corner of Clinton. There on the very edge of the sidewalk looms St. John's Episcopal Church, brandishing an imposing iron fence to discourage both devils and vandalizers. Here Darby stops.

Sarah's black dress is uncomfortably itchy and tight, not at all her size or style. Her coat is too long, her scarf too loud. She has no hat and her gloves are inadequate for even this short walk in the mid-winter wind. Suffocating under the gray flannel sky, she feels she is in someone else's life, perhaps a life belonging to the woman who owns this dress. But she is as curious as she is cold, as lucid as she is lost.

Darby opens the gate for her. As she passes, Sarah breathes through her nostrils the must of his corduroy jacket, the years he has worn it, even sees him as he selected it from the rack of many much like it. Men are strange, how they become attached to certain pieces of clothing, as she assumes he is to this jacket, as it is not heavy enough or appropriate for a church visit. She turns and wraps his scarf tighter around his neck, frees the mane of hair from beneath it—all this as if she were his wife of many years, tending to him with almost motherly care.

They enter through the center, massive oak door and are immediately overwhelmed by male voices and organ pipes, creating a richly mournful but jubilant blending of loss and salvation. This is the precise message. Sarah realizes that Darby has taken her to a funeral.

They slip into the last rear pew. There are ten pews left and right, an ornate, empty perch of a pulpit beyond that, and then more pews, the communion railing, the altar. A casket draped with a flag of many vibrant colors is parked in the center aisle. Sarah knows what that flag represents; she is a New Yorker and has seen it in parades, its rainbow colors also slapped proudly on bumperstickers. Crowding the church are statues of saints with sorrowful but grateful expressions, having already attained eternal life, as well as a great reputation here on earth. There is Christ with a lamb in his arms, and another Christ on the cross where he is shrouded in purple fabric from tortured head to pierced foot. It is now Lent. Sarah had only days before been crossed with ashes, nearly invisible on her ebony forehead. She looks again at the casket and its adornment. *What is Darby's connection to its contents?* There is no telling from his expression or any explanation given. He simply stares ahead, his bare hands curved around the weary oak of the pew in front of them.

Now and then heads turn back to them. They tilt slightly, wear sad smiles, or sometimes they shake subtly side to side. The singing ends abruptly and Sarah is left only with the stained light filtered through the high windows and the pervasive scents of cologne and incense. In this church—as in every church she's ever been in—lurks the nagging presence of all the unanswered prayers, all the pomp and praise, all the landmark baptisms, weddings, and funerals. This place, where so many lives begin and end.

Again, Sarah turns to Abraham Darby and sees that he has removed his cap, his hair matted down into its shape. Sarah fusses with it affectionately, forcing Darby finally to look at her. And there it is, his full age revealed. Every facial component is heavy and falling— brow, nose, cheeks, lips. Too much is revealed and she must look away.

A fairly young man climbs into the pulpit. Sarah remembers him from the restaurant last night, laughing through tears. He stumbles through his eulogy, but in a charming, naked way, lacking style or much confidence. He talks of Yago. Tells stories of Yago, the parent, the great dancer, the husband. Describes Yago's infectious laughter. He points at photographs, tells stories that mean nothing to Sarah, but as always in eulogies, there are tears and spontaneous, sharp rips of laughter. Yago Díaz, more talk of love, survival, human failings. It's all very romantic and dramatic and Sarah imagines herself in a theatre, at a play, and for all she knows, maybe it is just that.

But if it is, then Darby must be one of the actors; because once the younger man concludes, Darby stands and moves clumsily past her, then up the center aisle. Faces fat with anticipation swirl in his direction, as if he were a bride, ominous and transformed. Still in a dreamlike fog, as he begins the spiral ascent to the pulpit, Darby misjudges the very first step, falls forward and steadies himself with outstretched fingers on a higher step. But once he reaches the summit, he pulls himself up proudly to his full height. He has a churlish power, wild and unpredictable, intensified by his long Moses hair and demonic stare. In fact, the vitric blue of his eyes unsettles the assembled brethren and there is much fidgeting, whispering, and then one departure. Even the officiating priest seems uncomfortable, playing with the folds in his vestments and rudely consulting his watch.

Eventually, Abraham Darby takes a mess of papers from his jacket's inside pocket. He flattens them onto the podium and ceremoniously lays his hands on top of the pile, as though he could magically extract the words from the paper without looking.

Another man stands and leaves the church. As he passes Sarah, she clearly sees the anger in his face and something else. She thinks of a cloud heavy with a rain that refuses to fall. As she looks back at Darby, he seems a different man than the one she met last night, the man she'd slept with. Now he looks more like the avenging God. Yet she is clueless about what he will say, or even who it will be about. And then he speaks.

"You will excuse the random nature of my comments. I only wrote them last night and I was fairly drunk. My son. My son here before me, Yago...came into this world by accident and left the same way."

Sarah's eyes pop. *His son's funeral?*

"His mother is an artist, you probably know her, a painter from Costa Rica, whom I shared a life with many, many years ago. Yago was born of that rather random union, not in any nest of marriage or commitment or three-bedroom ranch in Hicksville. Alejandra and I lived as artists often do, self-obsessed, often irresponsible... creatures of impulse. She was twenty. I had no excuse.

"This little accident, our creation, Yago, became our new plaything and we made up a life for him." Darby has not yet consulted the papers he brought and appears to be addressing the blue-painted squares in the ceiling above, with each word as foreboding as the crumbling plaster edging each of these squares some 40 feet above them.

"That is until she split. I never did ask her to stay. I'm like most of you, content with quantity over quality. I just moved on to other women."

Rumbling in the funeral crowd now. Yet another man stands and leaves, forgetting his coat and being forced to return for it, somewhat diminishing the drama of his departure.

Darby smiles. "She took my son with her. He became her little travelling companion. Off they went to Costa Rica, to LA, to Mexico, into her new lives with new men, new women even. When I saw my son it was for only brief, awkward visits. When he was a teenager, mother and son settled back in Manhattan. Then I saw him much less. He was with *you*."

A long pause. His meaning not quite clear until...

"What we had not planned was that this golden-skinned, handsome and strong-boned young man, our best work of art, would become *perfect fodder* for the decadent bars of the meat market. It was like we raised him to send him off to war. A war inside his body. *Your war!*"

"Get off it, Darby!" an older man jumps to his feet, screaming. *"You turned your back on him!"* The woman next to him pulls him roughly back into his seat.

"This is my turn to talk," Darby shouts back. "He was my son. *My* son. What do you know?" He points at the previous speaker, as though he was an accusing attorney. "This one says that he was married to him. I never went to any wedding. He says he was a parent. I know there is a boy. But I barely know this boy. All I know for sure is that my son was a homosexual and the world he inhabited was a closed and closeted world. Closed not from fear or against bigotry. But no, closed by *choice* to exclude the rest of us!" Here he tosses his disregarded eulogy into the air.

"But what else was Yago? You know better than I do because you became his family, his friends, his lovers, his life. I am not homophobic. You all probably think I am. But his homosexuality was a roadblock he set. He stopped sharing his life with me when he joined this…culture? Lifestyle? Whatever you all call it. But I'll tell you something, if you ask me…"

Of course, no one is asking or wants him to continue.

"I was the one who didn't fit in. *A father has to fit into his son's life?*"

Sarah is not one to take on the embarrassment of another, but she is sinking into her seat, wishing he would sit back down. But there's something else she's feeling, beyond that, and she must search to unearth it. There is something in his vulnerability and misplaced anger that is heartbreaking, and yet appealing. He is at least exhibiting the courage to say what he really feels, as corrosive as it may sound.

"You all like to say that you have a right to choose whom you love," Darby continues. "So do I. I loved him." Then in a blubbering shout, "You are the ones who have now taken him from *me!*"

Sarah wonders if this could get worse. And then it does.

"Which one of you infected him? You can't possibly know, can you?" And again, screaming, *"Can you?"*

The priest rises and offers his hand up to Darby. "That is enough," he tells him kindly. "Please take your seat." Darby looks angry, confused, exhausted. He steps down and walks past the priest, pushing his hand out of his way.

✝ ✝ ✝

His gaseous, toxic words have darkened the flesh-colored walls of the church to the color of rotting cantaloupe. Sarah closes her mouth and blinks. She looks to her left and stares at yet another figure of Christ, laden down with purple fabric. She watches the tiny flames dancing in the green votives before it. Darby startles her. He is standing at the pew's end, glowering. She swings her legs to the side and he passes, then falls gracelessly into his seat.

She lays a hand over his balled fist. "That's not what I wrote," he tells her a bit too loudly. She has no words of consolation for him. The whole thing is too bizarre.

The funeral mass resumes and soon people tire of staring back at him. The choir belts out another hymn. Mouths shaped in unison display the precision and emotion of a military firing squad. These are sad and angry men and Sarah feels for them. Life is hard enough; let there be some grace in death.

Finally, it's over. Five men and a young boy maneuver the wheeled cart that the casket rests upon back down the center aisle towards the faint light of the open door. The first eulogist and the small boy man the front end of the cart. The older of the two slows the procession and stops the casket's progress right at Darby's pew. The man reaches into his blazer's inside pocket and hands Sarah a small white card. With the tiniest of smiles, he nods to her and then signals the resumption of the cortège.

Sarah holds the card on her open palm and there on it is another photograph of the smiling, beautiful, dark-haired man, Yago, *fodder for the meat market*. That is not what's printed; but rather beneath his lovely name of Yago Darby Díaz, she sees the tombstone dates:

April 2, 1971 – February 19, 2010

and printed beneath that:

"If it takes forever I will wait for you."

She thinks of the syrupy song…odd epitaph, but then her understanding of the deceased is only beginning to take form. Still the most compelling words on the card are handwritten, direct, and quite surprising:

Come with us to Turkuaz, Atlantic and Clinton. Bring him.
Johnny

CHAPTER FIVE • NOW PAINT FROM MEMORY

Back to Ash Wednesday

"With silence only as their benediction,
God's angels come,
Where, in the shadow of a great affliction,
The soul sits dumb."

John Greenleaf Whittier (1807–1892)

THE FIRST THING I NOTICED THAT WAS NEW WAS THAT I couldn't smell anything. There I was in that dingy, dirty hallway in a mess of antiseptics and spilled bodily fluids, I mean, how does this not stink to high heaven? Funny expression, right? Then when I ran my hands over what looked like stiff sheets and a nubby woven blanket, I realized that touch was also missing. I would have been alarmed at these observations, but there was also present in me an inability to feel much emotion, you know, like panic or just plain fear. I looked around the corridor and could make out the blur of nurses and folks pushing around other gurneys, but nobody paid any attention to me. But, like I said, I wasn't freaking out even though it was quite clear that I had died.

Now you're thinking that would be a pretty huge revelation but, to tell you the truth, I had felt it coming for some time. I don't know how a person feels death panting behind him like a wild, hungry animal, but I did. If you could ask a lot of dead folks if they felt it too, I bet they'd tell you absolutely yes. Unless you off yourself, you have no more idea of the day you'll die as you do the day you'll be born. But still, there are signs.

I didn't think it would be like this, but then who's going to tell you what will happen? I never bought into the white tunnel of light or the dude in the flowing robe with his team of lawyers at his side, ready to determine if you're heading north or south. I mean, I think I do believe in God, and I had been spending a little time lately thinking about what he's like and what he might make of me. But like most people, like you probably, over the course of my abbreviated life, I spent more time sitting on the john than thinking about God or any of this.

Just so you know, and I'm sure you're curious being that this is going to happen to each and every one of you, I wasn't smashed against the ceiling, looking down at the death scene and the wailing and all that. Well, there wasn't any wailing. But I was right there in my body. And thinking this was all a little weird, I just got off that gurney, got dressed, and walked towards the emergency room doors, the ones visitors use. A very hot little EMT even smiled at me and with a sweep of his hand allowed me to pass through first, so I wasn't invisible if that's what you're thinking. And I wasn't immune to a sharp little throb of lust, which was a great relief because that had been missing in my life for some time.

I know a great bar a few blocks from the hospital. It's a little sleazy but in a comforting way and I always see people who know me there. So I walked over in the cold rain, which for me was not a problem, being kind of in and out of body as I said. I never even got wet.

I did see Johnny running down the street and the rain made his hair look thinner than it already is. I was impressed with his speed and agility, though. I can't say I ever saw him really run full out like that.

He always kept Angelo's pace. He didn't notice me, which I was grateful for. I sure would have loved to hold him one last time, but I knew that a giant explosion of hysteria would certainly follow.

As I was walking to the bar, I wondered what was left for me, with most of my superficial desires and impulses stripped away, when I can't touch, smell, or feel anything intensely. *What was left for me?* I knew that was a big question. I sure didn't have the answer.

The place was a little sleepy; it was still early and the weather was so crappy. I pulled out my wallet and was amazed to see the amount of cash in there. Usually, if I have twenty bucks on me, I'm good. I generally only have to buy my first drink. But there packed in like a lobbyist's lunch fund was a fat deck of twenties! *How sweet is that?* I've heard of death benefits, but *please.* I pulled out a twenty and could barely shove the wallet into my back pocket and worried that my ass was going to look lopsided. I took a barstool and quite comfortably put my right cheek on the lump. No discomfort, like I explained.

I didn't see anybody I knew and the bartender was a new guy, but he came right over with what I usually, but not always, ordered. A Dos Equis and a shot of Patrón. He took my twenty and brought me back two more twenties. So I left him a twenty dollar tip. In my jacket pocket I discovered a fresh box of Sherman's, so I took the other twenty, stuck it into a candle on the bar, and lit one up. I threw the burning bill into an ashtray. Then I remembered that nowadays there are no ashtrays on bartops because smoking isn't permitted by law in establishments such as this, which I always thought was silly; it's not like this is a gym. People aren't here to get healthy. But nobody complained so I just enjoyed my smoke. I mean as best I could because it had no taste and even my tequila lacked heat or flavor.

I thought, maybe this is hell. You can have whatever you want, but you can't enjoy it. But then I did feel a nice little buzz in my head and ordered another round. There's hope.

I drank for hours and never saw a single person I knew. Some old guy did hit on me, but since I had plenty of money for drinks, I told him I wasn't interested, that I was married. He laughed. I guess he thought I was straight, but I don't know how anyone could think that. I told him I was married to a man and that we had a kid. He didn't laugh at that so I showed him a picture of Angelo and he told me he had a son, too. His son was in the army, in Afghanistan. I told him I hoped I wouldn't run into him soon. I doubt it, he said, he's not gay. You know what I meant.

A song came on that I like, but my head was feeling heavy and thick with all these crazy thoughts, so I didn't get off my stool to dance. Instead, I made a little pillow of my forearms and put my head there while that guy went on and on about his son and the war and how lonely he is. Maybe that's what put me out, or the drinks. I can't say.

What happened next you won't believe, but I'm not trying to convince you of anything. Just telling you what it was like for me and that this next thing surprised me, too.

After some time passed, and I don't know how much, I lifted my head up and the guy was still there with a young man in uniform, not that young really, maybe in his late thirties. Like me. My buddy had his arm around the soldier, whose uniform was dusty and I'm guessing the guy hadn't showered or shaved in quite a while. I was introduced but I didn't get his name. Everything seemed a little muffled and dreamy. But they both seemed happy and, catch this, I hopped off my stool and threw my arms around them both, pulled them tight into me, and I could feel the intense heat from their bodies. It was the first thing I had actually felt and I was absolutely elated.

CHAPTER SIX • PAYNE'S GRAY

Again, the Third Day After Ash Wednesday

THEN THERE IS JOHNNY. HAPPY, SILLY, LIGHTHEARTED Johnny Avitabile, whom you can't help but love, being so easygoing and comfortable to be around. He's like your favorite flannel shirt, the one from your early twenties with the button on the right cuff missing, the collar frayed, the blend of colors soothing. Johnny, master of the culinary sleight-of-hand, the good joke teller, the great friend. The Johnny who runs a small bistro on Court Street in Carroll Gardens and lives above it in a cozy, messy floor-through apartment that he shares with his son, Angelo, and until recently, with Yago.

In their life together, Johnny had played the perfect foil to his lover's moody, eruptive, sometimes insular nature. But on his good days, which were many, Yago had been the spice that made their life together like an endless trip to Disneyland. Being so childlike himself, the idea of bringing a baby into their lives had seemed to Yago like gaining a new playmate.

Johnny had been the better—really, only—choice for biological father to Angelo, not simply because of his pragmatic and disciplined nature, but because he was HIV negative.

Johnny is the type of parent who gets genuinely excited about play-dates in Carroll Street Park, lunching with other parents there, and supervising homework. Yago parented differently, utilizing his rich imagination to create for Angelo a tantalizing and magical world far beyond Brooklyn. They would lose themselves in tales of dragons, those they slay and those they befriend. Angelo adored them both and would brag about his two fathers, feeling sorry for those with only one.

But all that has changed. Johnny now stands face to face with Yago's father at Turkuaz, the popular Turkish restaurant on Atlantic Avenue. Johnny is still in his heavy coat with his hands dangling at his side. Darby towers over him; and judging from his expression and habit, Johnny knows he won't be staying long.

Johnny hadn't been fazed by Darby's incendiary rant. "You have every right to say what you feel at your son's funeral," he tells him now. "I'm sure you didn't offend *him*. Anyway, words don't make him any more or less gone."

Darby looks bewildered, somehow deflated.

"I know you loved Yago," Johnny adds.

Darby reinflates. "You have no idea what I feel."

"Yes, of course. I don't. I barely know what I feel. Excuse me, Abe, the bar is calling me."

Sarah has just returned from checking her coat and when summoned, follows Johnny to the bar, a separate room one must pass through before entering the core dining area. He nods towards a stool next to him and says, "Bet you'd like a big fat drink."

As he waits patiently for the bartender, she observes that something is amiss in his proportions. The head, neck, hands, the thickness of his limbs, all belong to a much taller man; his long, thinning hair belonging to an older face. Still, his eyes are as clear and bright as a boy's and he has an impish smile that she finds quite disarming. He smells of cigarettes and something else. *What is it?* A spice possibly, something like cinnamon or clove.

"He's not easy. You must know that," he says. "I shouldn't have called him Abe. He hates that. He prefers *Dahby*. Darby is how he signs his work, how he's referred to in the Arts and Leisure section of the *Times*. Even Yago calls him Darby. Called. I doubt that you call him Abe."

"I've barely used his name. I really don't know him at all. We just met...yesterday."

"Really? And you tag along to his son's funeral. I'm sorry...that came out wrong. I mean it's not much of a second date." He turns away. "Could we have two cosmopolitans, please. Grey Goose." And back at her, almost flirtatiously, "Good by you, my enigmatic lady?"

"I'm easy."

"Oh, don't tell me too much. You know he is my father-in-law."

As they wait silently, wrapped safely in the conversational noise around them, Johnny catches a few quick glimpses of her in the gaudy neck scarf, the tall brown boots with the *black* dress. The frock is too short in the sleeves, too tight in the bust *(darts unflatteringly north of the bosom!)*, and neither fashionably short nor long. *Something ain't right.*

"Is this a borrowed dress?" he asks as the drinks arrive.

Sarah takes a healthy swallow. "Yes. Whose I don't know. You think it doesn't suit me?"

"I don't know your style but my guess is this ain't it."

She smiles. Doesn't respond.

He brings his lips to his drink and slurps like a child. He looks at her again and tries to picture her in a wildly colorful, wraparound Africany thing, something to offset her oversized, podlike eyes. Can't help liking her sexy mouth. He wonders how old she is and how she came to accompany the caveman, Abe.

Sarah squirms atop her stool. "You're Yago's partner, I assume. We haven't introduced ourselves."

"You assume incorrectly. Yago and I are actually married. Did it again. *Were* married legally in the state of Massachusetts. My idea. Maybe not my *best* idea given his roaming nature. Anywho, I'm a widower now." He pushes his hair from his face. "Wasn't on my list of things to do. Name is Johnny. Johnny Avitabile, Brooklyn, New York, born, raised, still reside."

"Sarah Obadias. Upper Upper West Side." Another healthy swallow. "You seem to be handling things so well."

"That's because I'm not alone right now. I've been packing people around me like horny straight guys around a belly dancer. That reminds me! They have really fabulous belly dancers here. Girls *and* some very hunky guys."

"I am not intruding, I hope?"

"You are certainly not. You know what they say about funerals, the more the merrier. Or is it bore the burier? Or sore the carrier? I forget, but I'm glad you're here. The old man needs backup." Johnny takes the thin neck of his glass, touches the rim with his lower lip, and this time, neatly as an injection, directs the entire contents down his throat. Waves for two more.

"Tell me about your son. That was your son, yes? The smallest pallbearer."

He lowers his head, brings his hands together, then places them against his chest. Looks to Sarah. "Amidst the sooty snow and colorless sky, our boy Angelo is the improbable red rose that freezes in bloom and remains vibrant, brightening even the darkest days of February, such as now. To me, he is even more perfect than my red velvet cake, a happy blend of my wildly affectionate and Yago's playful natures. Angelo is five, the world his toy, prefers to sleep on the floor, loves lemons and those nasty yellow peppers in a jar. He's a great dancer, like his Papa, loves disco. Keeps asking me where is Papa and when will he get back. I tried to explain heaven, but it sounded so much like the fairy tales we read that I gave up. So I finally told him the truth. I don't know.

"Wanna meet Angelo? I'm sorry, I already forgot your name."

"Sarah. I'd love to meet him. He's here?"

"Tucked away in the kitchen. Let's find him!" Johnny tosses down the first half of his second drink, then takes both their glasses with him.

Beneath the tent-like, fabric ceiling of the main dining room, they make their way through groups of laughing mourners, their glasses reflecting the light from the abundance of candles on the linen tablecloths. Circles of artificial light on the polished wooden floor guide their path as hands reach for Johnny's arm and quiet settles on each group as he approaches. "I am so sorry" and "If there's anything I can do" flutter past him and he smiles each time, squeezing flesh in thanks. Sarah trails behind him like an oversized caboose, collecting questioning looks and appraisals. The unlikely widower keeps running his hands through his long, dark hair, combing it off his forehead, freeing it from his shirt collar. At room's end he turns his head slightly and quietly tells Sarah, "I cannot wait for this to be over. Do you think any of them are talking about Yago?" He turns completely around, facing her, smirking. "Hey, maybe I'm wrong. He's slept with half of them."

When the kitchen doors swing wide, Sarah is accosted by a sensory overload. The lights are blindingly bright and the room's air wiggles with heat. Trays of grilled meats, charred shrimp, stuffed baby eggplants, and bowls of hummus and baba ghannouj fly by them. Sarah stares in a ravenous way as they pass, causing Johnny to cry out, "Somebody make her a plate!" Within minutes, plates for both arrive and Johnny leads her to a far corner of the kitchen and to a small boy sitting on top of a stainless steel cart. He has long golden curls and enormous dark eyes, looking to Sarah more a caricature of a child than a living, breathing one. They both find spaces for plates and glasses, and as they approach the boy, he stills his swinging feet when he gets a glimpse of Johnny. His small face is covered in honey and pastry, but still his father takes him in his arms and presses his unshaven cheek against his son's. When Johnny turns to Sarah, she smiles at the sticky, flaky crumbs littering his stubble.

"Angelo, may I present my new friend…"

"Reverend Obadias," Sarah interrupts and extends her hand. She does not approve of children addressing adults by their first names.

"Oh." Johnny draws out this single word for a full three seconds, keeping his lips in a tight little circle as his eyes roam the ceiling in concentrated thought. "Oh my, my, my. Kinda like Judas dating Mary Magdalene, I mean like, you know, after she repented."

"Not exactly. More like Judas dating the devil, I suppose."

The boy cautiously takes Sarah's hand in both of his, then runs his sticky fingers over her soft skin. "Hello," he says, a little unsure as to what to make of this tall brown woman with bright red lips. "I like your boobies" is all he musters.

"Shit!" Johnny takes the boy in his arms abruptly, fearing Angelo might reach out and touch the minister's breasts. "Oh, sorry I said that. And sorry he said *that*."

"He will learn soon enough not to speak his mind so freely," Sarah says. "Until then, thank you, Angelo, for the compliment. Most males are not so straightforward."

The boy looks confused but is quickly distracted by what Sarah pulls from a surprise pocket in the side of her dress. She hands him the crumpled holy card of the pleading Christ.

"What do you say, Angelo?" Johnny prompts.

Angelo holds it close to his eyes, flips the card over and then back again. "Thank you?"

"Do you know who that is?" Sarah asks.

"Jesus. It's Jesus. He's sad. He's saying his prayers. I think he doesn't want to."

"Angelo goes to Sunday school. Loves it, really," his father says. "Don't you, sweetie?"

"You're right, Angelo. Jesus is very sad and probably doesn't want to be praying right then," Sarah explains, but the boy has already squirmed away from Johnny's arms and has dropped the holy card on the floor. He investigates the food on his father's plate, dipping his messy little fingers into the hummus, then nabbing parsley-flecked white beans and cubes of the blackened lamb.

Johnny picks up the holy card. "I'll keep this for him." He takes another long sip from his cocktail, and then pulls a stool over for the minister.

"Please join us. I promise not to eat off your plate."

She sits, eats. "This is wonderful. I didn't realize how hungry I was."

"You Baptist?"

"Because I'm black folk?"

"Just a question."

"Not Baptist, not so conservative. Let's just say a fairly liberal denomination that encourages women to join the ministry. I'm an Associate Pastor, on sabbatical. Or that's what we agreed to call it. And you? Wait, you're gay so I'll go with the stereotype, too. A Unitarian Universalist and in the theatre?"

"Partially correct! I'm a runaway Catholic that's taken up with the Episcopalians. I like their Sunday school. I do have a sort of stage. That's my restaurant. Not a great dad job, hours-wise, but our home is right above it. Angelo spends a lot of time in the restaurant's kitchen…even has his own little cot in the corner."

"Is this your place?"

"God, no. I have a tiny place on Court Street, not far from our church. We do come here a lot. And this place is large enough to handle all of Yago's friends. He was very popular. You've seen the pictures of him, right?"

Of course she has; they were everywhere, at the funeral and here, as well. Paintings on easels, photo montages on corkboard, sketches laid out on tabletops—all homage paid to the bon vivant, the son of painters, friend to barhops and past lovers, the family man.

"He was a beautiful man," she says simply. She had been unnerved by the intense sensuality in his soft eyes and full mouth, contrasted and accentuated by his father's sharper, Nordic features. Still, those eyes never seem truly focused and even when laughing, he appears distracted, sullen.

"Are those all Darby's paintings of him?" she asks Johnny.

"Well, the whimsical and playful ones, when he was a kid mostly, those are watercolors painted by his mother. The large oils that are rather dark and detached, those are Darby's."

Angelo has finished eating and is tugging on Johnny's sleeve, wanting to leave.

"Just a second, my son. Yago loved his mother's paintings, but was very confused by his father's portraits, which were mostly done from memory or photographs. Rarely with him in the room. Isn't that weird?"

"Then why are they here?"

"Because I love them. I picked them out yesterday, at his loft. I know they're not really Yago, but…" Angelo is getting more persistent, tugging harder. "Angelo, stop! Where's Allyssa? She should be watching you." Again to Sarah, "Allyssa's our personal angel. I'm sorry, where was I? Oh, I love those paintings because they're so darkly emotional, but more the painter's emotion, not the subject's."

"Is that emotion love?" she asks.

"No. Loss. Or maybe longing. But I think, they are really beautiful. Yago thought so, too."

‡ ‡ ‡

Johnny smokes the one cigarette that Allyssa had authorized. He has given her the unenviable task of rationing. So he smokes it with great intent, inhaling deeply, exhaling slowly. He wears only his old-fashioned, unstylish tweed blazer with a flimsy v-neck sweater and oxford shirt beneath. It's dark now and chilly in the courtyard behind the restaurant.

He feels his anger towards Yago gurgling in his stomach, trying to push its way into his chest. "Yago is dead," he says. Then he tries it with a British accent, very formally, as if to a war widow: "Yes, I am afraid Yago is dead. He was lost in battle, trying to save himself. No medal for that. So sorry."

Not funny, he tells himself. More long drags on the cigarette. He had had to call people, explain what had happened. Long distance to Alejandra. A short distance to close friends. A brief conversation with Darby. Awful. That was the worst. No, Angelo was the worst. Johnny could kick himself for the way he did it. "Papa went away. He's an angel, now." How stupid! *Yago, an angel?*

Thank God Allyssa had arranged for the funeral, made more calls, got this restaurant. How it will be paid for he has no idea. He wanted to ask Darby for help but chickened out.

What had Darby said at the service? Johnny tries to remember his exact words...something inane like my son came into this world by accident, left the same way. And then, meanspiritedly, calling him fodder for the meat market. *Asshole.*

He grinds out the cigarette with his shoe. Shoes Yago hated, being too worn, too last-century. "They look like my father's," he'd said. But sometimes Yago dressed like a male prostitute, Johnny remembers. Tight, faded jeans, mesh shirts. *C'mon! Mesh shirts?*

Well, that little speech of Darby's sure pissed off a lot of people, but not him. Of course, he didn't like all the homophobic vitriol, but he already knew that he felt that way. It didn't offend him. There were some pretty right-on observations in all that dung. It didn't bother him when he dismissed their marriage ceremony, the baptism of their son. He was invited to both, but refused to go. He's just Darby. Darby will never change. Yago didn't care. At least that's what he said. And Alejandra was always there. Will always still be there for them.

Johnny looks up at the rectangle of sky above him, murky and starless, a sad little postage stamp representing the whole of the cosmos. He can feel the temperature dropping and wraps his arms around himself. Yago always came home, always slept with him, would even drape his long arms around Johnny if Johnny asked him to. *Who would do that now?* Who could possibly ever take the place of this beautiful, fucked-up man he has loved for so long? Even the pretense of fidelity and romance is better than nothing at all.

Here it is, Johnny realizes, the perfect chance to cry. Alone, cold, with a dismal bank account, lackluster business, a son to raise without Yago. Eight million minus one in these five boroughs now. It's surprisingly quiet behind the restaurant on crazy Atlantic Avenue, where people dine on Japanese, Italian, Turkish or Lebanese food, all within a single block on this typical Saturday night. Knowing he is alone amidst so many mindlessly happy revelers makes it so much worse. He has been abandoned. That's how it feels. *Here one day, gone the next. Unbelievable.*

In the stillness, broken only by humming exhaust fans, Johnny squeezes his dry eyes shut. It's that churning anger that keeps the tears away. He doesn't want to go deeper than that. *Why go looking for pain?* Anger will do just fine.

But even the anger is muddied with the numbness he feels. *God I wish I had another cigarette.* No. *God, don't let me stop feeling!* That should be what he prays for. So he traipses through his Grey Goose–saturated head, past his fragile heart, and attempts to locate the chakras he never really got during his total two weeks of yoga. All the way down to the soles of his unfashionable shoes, and still he finds nothing. For his little boy? Right now all words, all habit. He can't locate the deep emotion he knows is somewhere. For Allyssa with the golden hair and cherub face? *Where is at least gratitude?*

He runs his hands over his arms, his chest, across his stomach, squeezes his buttocks, then his knees.

"Am I interrupting something?" Sarah is magically standing next to him. She hands him a cigarette. "Allyssa gave me two. You are not to ask for more. Sweet girl."

She lights his with a match, and then her own.

"You smoke?" He wanted it to sound more casual, but it slipped out accusatorially.

"No. You?"

"Absolutely not. Bad habit."

They inhale and exhale almost in unison, their backs against the building. There are tables but no chairs in the winter courtyard.

"Allyssa wants to take Angelo home. He fell asleep on a countertop."

Why Sarah feels so familiar, like family, Johnny can't say, but her company right now is soothing. "I'll check on Angelo in a few minutes. You met Allyssa?"

"So what happened to Yago?" she asks, and he stiffens. *Yes, she is even annoying like family.*

"He had a fatal heart attack Wednesday night. He was found on the street in the Village. I don't know who he was with or where he was coming from or going. They said it was a heart attack so I have to believe it was.

"People think AIDS is over. It's not. He was on antiretrovirals for a long, long time. That was probably part of the cause. He also has...had...a lot of bad cholesterol in his blood. He was only 38."

Sarah awkwardly drapes an arm around his neck and pulls him closer. They are side by side, like teammates, but he takes a long drag on his cigarette and throws it down, breaking free.

"He was already dead when I got to the hospital. He always hated long goodbyes. I just sat there in a folding chair next to the gurney in the hallway, not even a room, touching his face, his gorgeous curls, his chest. I guess they had cleaned him up but his face was cut and bruised. His chest, too. They told me he had fallen down some steps, they supposed, you know, after the heart attack.

"The hospital staff was kind, said I could stay with him as long as I liked. I left after a few minutes. Signed some papers, then stood outside, staring at nothing, consciously remembering to breathe, not knowing what to do next."

He picks up the cigarette butt from the ground, examining it for reuse. "I went kinda numb. There was a lot to do. Calling people, his mom Alejandra, Darby, saying the same words over and over. And every time I still couldn't believe it myself."

"I can see you love your son."

Johnny is losing patience. "I know I do. Hey, I'm sure you mean well, but..." He opens the back door to leave, but she stops him.

"Wait." Sarah places her palm against the cold metal and gently pushes the door closed.

"I should get back," he says.

"Maybe I can help you," she says without much conviction.

"I doubt it. I'm feeling by rote."

"That's normal." Sarah reaches for his hand but he backs away further into the courtyard.

"Listen. I don't feel normal," he barks. "Our relationship wasn't your normal relationship. It was always changing. He'd get too close and get antsy and quiet and pull away. Then he'd be back, all silly and sweet. He was as affectionate as he could be, and faked it when he wasn't feeling that way. He had no job other than bartending from time to time. Nothing grounded him. I'd see Angelo try. Angelo adored him the way a child longs for something that is just out of reach. I know he loved us. I know he loved me...and our son.

"Anyway, I don't need a minister. Don't need the pep talk for the grief-stricken."

"Fair enough, Johnny. What do I know?" She walks over to him and they both take another long look at the rectangle of night sky above. "Just one more thing and I'll leave you alone. Tell me...I'm curious...who is Angelo's mother? Is she in the picture?"

If he's annoyed, he doesn't show it; the change of subject welcome. "Honestly, I'm freezing. You've met her, in the kitchen. The angel with the stash of smokes."

"Allyssa? Yes, of course. He has her hair and playful eyes."

"I asked her to do this for me. Or with me. Any way she wanted it to be. I wanted a child so badly. And just guessing, but I bet you're curious how we made him. And I'll tell you. It was the old-fashioned way."

"Intercourse?"

"Spoken like a true, doctrine-up-the-wazoo minister." But he smiles, as if to erase the insult. "Yep, the old in-and-out. Many times." He comes closer and tilts his head upward so they're as eye to eye as possible. Sarah chucks her head backward, as if dodging an oncoming kiss.

"And now I'm going to tell you something I've never told anybody. Not even Allyssa."

Sarah turns her head, not because he's shocking her by his frank talk, but in hopes that her breaking away might make the telling easier for him.

But he repositions himself to be, again, right in her face. His eyes are wide and he looks a little crazy.

"I liked it! I mean really liked it, and it was the first time with a girl. We made it fun. First a movie, then we'd cook up a little something in the kitchen, and then cook up a little something in the sack. My body surprised me. I became a little baby-making machine. And Allyssa! In bed, she's what they mean by a truly natural woman."

"Looking out on the morning rain…" Sarah sings, looking away from his wild-eyed stare.

Johnny settles, smiles. "I used to feel so…uninspired…"

"And when I knew I had to face another day…"

"Lord, it made me feel so tired."

"Hey, Johnny, you've got a great voice."

"Well, I'm a gay man. You know, glee club, piano bars, show tunes. And back at you!"

"Well, I'm a black woman. You know, gospel hymns, freedom marches, show tunes."

"Can we go in now?" he whines. "I can't feel my fingers or my toes."

"Yeah, sure," Sarah says, but adds as they again reach the door, "so you're bisexual?"

"Hell no! See, that's what you people…"

"You people?" she interrupts.

They've entered the chaos of the kitchen now. "I mean straight people. Lots of gays and lesbians can get it on with members of the opposite sex. There's no biological defect or anatomical roadblock. It's all about who you fall in love with, dream about, walk into walls over. And that would be Yago for me. That's who made me walk into walls, although I have to admit the sex thing had kind of faded as of late. But you people always make it only about sex. Is that how it is with you?"

She's inspired to be honest. "Sometimes." She's certainly not in love with Darby, but last night, well that was definitely about sex.

Johnny takes her hand, and as they wind through the shouting and darting bodies of a still busy kitchen, he whispers in her ear, "Tell me that you have *never* thought about lying down with a woman?" He tilts his head like an inquisitive puppy and then they rejoin the festivities of the après funeral.

Beneath the medieval-looking, hanging light fixtures, the crowd is in a gyrating, fluid state, very animated, congregating around the two promised belly dancers, one female, one male. The music is richly textured, exotic, and highly erotic. Tables still brimming with delicacies have been pushed to the side and everyone is dancing, smiling, even the awakened Angelo, legs dangling, in the arms of Allyssa. Some men are bare-chested except for the neckties bisecting their chests.

Central in the circus-like room is an eery, life-sized painting of Yago and a wooden table heaped with Yago memorabilia—photos, sketches, some jewelry, a stocking cap, a deck of cards, an ornate cross, and a stack of comic books.

"Allyssa told people to bring things that reminded them of Yago. The comic books are from Angelo. That was their thing," Johnny tells Sarah as they look through the treasures. "He was Angelo's comic book hero, flat and wonderful."

Sarah senses his resilient anger but does not react to it. She scans the room for signs of Darby, but Johnny grabs her hand and awkwardly twirls her body into his. Though she's much taller, their bodies press nicely together and off they go in some odd Turkish waltz.

If this is mourning, Sarah wonders, *what would celebrating look like?*

CHAPTER SEVEN • TRANSPARENT EARTH YELLOW

DARBY HAD WAITED OUTSIDE IN THE WET FEBRUARY COLD, huddled like a homeless man against the restaurant's face. No one had looked at him or spoken to him, not strangers or even those who had likely recognized him as they left the party. And yes, to him it had seemed a party, a raucous hoopla to mark the death of his son.

He had been ignored, become agitated, grown impatient. He left. Had taken the subway back to Tribeca. Extricated his decrepit Cadillac from the overpriced lot. Driven back to Atlantic Avenue. Had cupped his hands around his eyes, peered inside. Watched her dance. *Dancing? It's a fucking wake!*

He sits now, double-parked, waiting. Fingers the soft fibers of her sweater, which he had stuffed into a plastic bag with the rest of her clothing. So hungry now. Leaves the car there with flashers on, gets a slice of pizza two doors down. Too hot. Waits, watching his abandoned car. Consumes the pizza in five bites. Thirsty now. "Coke, please. Large."

"Only Pepsi."

Sucks down half. Returns to the car. Belches. Up and out again, to the restaurant's window. She's holding the boy. Face to face they are. Boy's fingers trace her lower lip. Darby remembers those lips.

Remembers other things. Can't really believe it's the same woman. She gives the boy to Johnny in exchange for her coat.

Darby walks to the entrance. Opens the door and there she is. Wraps his arms clumsily around her. Whispers, "I need to be near the water. I have a house out on the East End. Couple of hours' drive. Will you do one more thing for me?"

"I have nothing," Sarah tells him. "Not even a toothbrush."

"I'll buy one for you." He leads her to the car, opens her door.

"We need to talk, Darby."

"Yeah, I know. We will."

He drives. Soon they're under the carcass of the Brooklyn Bridge. Then, his favorite view of Lower Manhattan. Here the suspension-destroying terrain of the Brooklyn-Queens Expressway. Then the Long Island Expressway, surprisingly empty for a Saturday evening, not all that late.

Radio on. Uptown jazz station he favors. A balm. Maybe Coleman Hawkins. Yes, him. Another garlicky belch. No apology needed as she sleeps, or seems to. Dashboard lights paint her in soft blues. She lies, buried beneath her coat, over the corduroy jacket he had gallantly thrown down. Her head, surprisingly heavy on his thigh, body curved to fit. Can't be comfortable. Maybe she drank enough not to care.

Darby cups her head with his hand. Looks funny this hand, like it's not his, a clean white even in the dim light; he thinks of snow in bright moonlight. He pets her tiny silvery curls. Then his fingertips stroke the nape of her neck. She responds with a moaning sigh. They enter Nassau County.

The hypnotic flashing of headlights from oncoming traffic lulls him into a calmer, reflective state. He is driving away, heading east with a woman. A light rain falls that is barely more than mist. Hartman and Coltrane together on the crappy car radio. All familiar. He strains to hear the comforting sounds of tires on wet pavement, her gentle breaths. All knowable.

But from the seat directly behind him comes a pressure on his back, not a blow, but a heavy leaning. Then, a whispering rush of warm air into his right ear, followed by a deep inhalation, then another slow exhalation and the putrid smell of fermentation.

His right hand jerks aloft from Sarah's head and both hands tighten onto the steering wheel. A wet heat emanates from behind him as dense as August sea air. Darby's heartbeat thuds an irregular rhythm and sweat soaks his hairline. He flips off the radio.

Silence. A messy, frightening silence laden with anticipation. Darby senses the presence of someone behind him, perhaps a child. Perhaps it is his. There is that smell, sweetness and salt, the one that never leaves a child, will always be familiar to a parent. A marker. *Or is it pure fatigue conjuring up an impossible passenger?*

The sleeping stranger and the man yearning for his son drive on in an old car packed with painful memories. Darby experiences all that is beyond his Cadillac as an abstract painting, the wisps of passing cars, the hazy blocks of strip malls, the uncomfortably bright orange on a Home Depot sign, the thick dabs of housing and lines of head-lights, a false yellow spilling randomly across the canvas. Then when deeper into Suffolk County, the highway becomes edged in dark blotches of shrubby pines with a murky gouache of sky overhead. All elements seem detached and unrelated.

Because this is just a dream, of course. Yes, he thinks, this whole sequence—the phone call, the dinner at Malatesta, her, the sex, the funeral, this drive east—all but an odd dream, chockfull of the usual fears and common anxieties. *What had he read?* Simply stare at your open palm before sleep and recall it while dreaming. Consciously look at it. Touch it with your other hand. This controlling act will allow you to enjoy the bizarre elements of the dream, even alter them. *Because it is only a dream.*

So Darby stares at his right palm. He opens and closes his hand three times. Turns the radio on, now a dreary soft rock station, and then off. Accelerates. Rests his palm on the hip of his sleeping passenger. Feels so reassuring. He is not bothered by the eery, shallow panting in the back seat. He does not object to the occasional light touch upon his right shoulder, in his hair. A child's touch, loving, exploratory.

Darby, emboldened by knowing he is likely dreaming, looks in the rearview mirror and sees the head of a boy, wet hair plastered against his skull. A small hand dusted with sand comes to rest again on his right shoulder.

His Cadillac hits a pothole hard and he looks at the road ahead and then at his speedometer. He's doing 80. Slows to 50. Shadows are everywhere, and seeping into the interior of the car so he can barely see. He knows he should pull over, but his visceral response to all of this is to flee. He must keep moving.

Darby does know the boy and his age, though his form is not well-defined. It is the boy they almost lost, the one who had been swimming in the pre-storm roughness of the Sound, the boy who had disappeared into a wave and only reappeared as a sandy, flat mass on the shore's edge minutes later, while Darby had flailed ineffectually in the surf. The sea had spit the child back, being too young, too unsubstantial to consume.

Yes, it *is* this boy, his boy. His long curls drip chilling sea water down Darby's neck. There's the boyhood smell of him, their soap, his perspiration, the complex sweetness. *Unmistakable.*

It isn't until they've left the Expressway—the dreaming woman, the almost drowned boy, his negligent father—and are travelling further east on the North Road that Darby is able to speak. "Are you only a memory? I don't believe in ghosts."

No response. Perhaps, Darby thinks, he only thought the words.

"Who *are* you?" He needs verification, even if this visitation is only the product of fatigue and grief.

"You have no idea?" *A man's voice!*

"Who *are* you? Is it you, Yago?"

"Who are *you?*"

"Stop answering questions with questions!" Darby sees two deer only a few yards from the road, near the wood's edge. He flashes his high beams but they ignore him, and continue nibbling, heads bent. *Maybe it is him who isn't really here!*

"Stop questioning answers," he hears from the back seat.

"You're playing games with me," Darby says. His own voice seems warbled and muffled.

"We've always played games," comes the imagined reply, now softer, boyish.

"Games?" Darby asks.

"Yes. You were good at games."

"And now?" Darby searches the rearview mirror, but sees nothing. He is tempted to turn around, but decides against it. "And now?" he repeats.

"I am better."

"Stay with me," Darby says.

"It's difficult. A thin line separates me from you, my staying from my leaving," he tells his father.

Darby grows impatient. He is not a man comfortable with the hogwash of new age sensibilities. This smacks of all that, dream or not. "At least tell me you love me, goddammit," he demands.

"Darby?" Sarah wakes. "What did you say?"

But Darby has nothing to say, until "I think I fell asleep."

"While driving? Why didn't you wake me up?" Sarah sits up, straightens her dreadful, itching dress, pulls her boots on. He does look like he's just woken from a nightmare, bug-eyed and sweaty. "Are you alright?" she asks.

"We need to stop and pick up some food," Darby says.

She cracks her window and takes in the heavy, salty air. She sees a movie theater, closed for the season, and small shops and restaurants. The village is nearly void of life.

"Where are we?"

"Well, we're either in some dark Brecht play or it's Greenport," Darby says as he pulls into a space near a corner market. Two Hispanic men in heavy plaid jackets stand near the door, drinking from paper cups; one is smoking.

"Wait here," Darby instructs. He leaves the car running, flips the radio on, so she won't be lonely. He tunes to a local station. More jazz, but smoother, hipper.

Cold air greets him. He pulls his wallet from his back pocket. Eighteen bucks. *Shit.* Knows they don't take credit. Eighteen will have to do. Picks up milk, eggs, bread, an onion, an orange, a scrap of cheese, keeping track of the total in his head. Finds Sarah a cheap toothbrush.

The clerk can't find a price on the toothbrush. Out comes a huge binder filled with invoices.

Darby looks out to the car, but Sarah is no longer in the passenger seat. *Has she been abducted by the apparition in the back seat?* He should have checked back there. Maybe she just wandered off, piled into another stranger's car.

Darby slaps his eighteen dollars onto the countertop. "Keep the change…if there is any. I gotta go." The cheese, onion and orange are dropped into trouser pockets, toothbrush clamped between his teeth, the rest stacked in his hands.

Away from the Cadillac, Sarah turns up her collar. There's a phone pressed against her ear.

"Mama, it's late. Are you alright?" A voice traveling from another world.

"Oh, I'm fine, Baby," Sarah replies. "I'm just…going away for the weekend."

"Where? You never mentioned a trip."

"Well, it wasn't really planned. Gracie, listen. Have you ever gone to a late afternoon movie, a really good one, really engrossing? It takes you somewhere else. You come out of the theatre and it's still daylight and you have absolutely no idea what your life is about."

"You were at a movie? I'm not following you, Mom."

"No, no. I just met someone who…"

"Who you're spending the weekend with? A complete stranger!"

"Baby, no. I mean, yes. He was a stranger. Different than anyone I've ever met."

"As in white."

"Ah, yes. He is white. Actually, almost entirely white. Somehow I got drawn into his life…at an insanely emotional moment. Honey, he has just lost his son. I didn't know that at first. My thoughts keep coming back to you. How very much you mean to me, help to define me in many ways. Well, you're a mother. You know what I'm saying."

"At least now you're starting to sound like you. This is none of my business, but, Mama, did you sleep with this very white man? You and Daddy aren't even divorced. You slept with him, didn't you? I cannot believe this."

"You are correct. This is none of your business and certainly not your father's. Listen, I have no idea if I'll ever see him after this. Not even sure if I want to. I'm not sure about a lot of things these days. Grace, I have to go. I have my phone. For God's sake, don't worry about me."

He waits in the car until Sarah snaps her phone shut and walks back to him. Emboldened by her return he checks the back seat, but there is no one. The seat does looks wet. Could have been wet already.

"Just a bit longer," he says, and she smiles. "One hopes," she replies, "one always hopes for more time."

He finds the comment odd but says nothing. She may have been referring to their own mortality but *who wants to talk about that?* More time. One always hopes for more time. As he drives, he remembers the thin line his dream son had talked about. Or whoever that was who had so little to say. *There are always lines; this is not a revelation.* He had hoped for more should the dead speak. But that line he spoke of, Darby knew he could paint it, make it real. It would be a pale blue.

He is a practical man, holds a pragmatic work ethic, even when working through dreams. Works impulsively but methodically on his paintings. Generally eats the same foods day to day. Actually quite conservative in matters of politics and ethics. All Norwegians on his mother's side. His father a nonpracticing Russian Jew. *That is who he is and he pretends to be no more.* But there is, always has been, one exception to his predictable ways; this he freely admits. Concerning sex, fidelity, relationships with women, he has always been loose and noncommittal. It's not that he wanted every woman he met; it's just that he had never wanted just one.

He feels it is not entirely his fault that he has no moral convictions when it comes to sex…or even religion. He was not raised in any particular faith and none attracted him as an adult. Never saw the need. If he had to describe his spiritual beliefs, he'd have to say he believes in God, though doesn't know him personally. Maybe it's the act of painting that comes closest to meditation and prayer, he consoles himself. Then he is tapped into something greater than himself. He decides that he will paint that blue line between heaven and earth, life and death. See where that takes him.

"What do *you* make of death?" Darby asks Sarah, as though she were compliant in his wandering thoughts.

"God Almighty! Where on earth did that come from?" Sarah stares at his profile.

"How can I not be thinking about it? My only child has died. You know, I almost lost him once many years ago. He nearly drowned out here, in the Sound. He was there, splashing around, throwing his tiny body into the shore-breakers, and then he was gone. I couldn't find him, Sarah. Many minutes passed and I couldn't find him."

"But he survived."

"With no help from me. Found him up on the beach. The sea saved him, not me. I'd been miserable; I don't even remember why. Drank most of the afternoon. Do you know how vast the sea can look when it's churning, the same color as the sky, and one small boy is lost in it?"

"Remember Genesis, Darby? The child sacrifice? Fate threatened him and some passing angel came to the rescue. Think of it that way."

"Where was that angel last Wednesday?" Darby asks angrily. He stares at the road, shaking his head.

"Well, anyway, I don't fear death," Sarah says, allowing the conversation to return to its original dark path. "It's life that looms large. I feel I have time. I don't feel old. My knees are a mess. My hands are knotted with arthritis. I've lost somewhere an inch and a half. But I feel I have time. I need time."

Darby pulls the car to the side of the street. Sarah takes her new scarf and wraps it over her head like a peasant. Because he looks so lost, she adds, "I'll look after you another night, if that's what you need."

"We're here," he says. "This is it."

Sarah steps from the overheated interior of his car into the brisk sea air. She sees that they are on a dead-end road with the water roaring not far beyond. To her left stands a small two-story, white clapboard house with many windows. A cracked terra cotta planter spills last summer's dead annuals onto the front steps. Sarah has never lived in a house, but this one is strangely appealing.

She takes the eggs and the carton of milk from him and they walk together to the house. "Is this yours?"

"I'm sorry, what?"

"This lovely little house, is it yours?"

Darby struggles with both groceries and words. "Been in the family forever. Now belongs to…just me and…really, my sister, too. But she never comes here. It's a place Yago always loved."

"It's charming. Is it heated?"

CHAPTER EIGHT • BURNT OATMEAL BROWN

JOHNNY AVITABILE FALLS ON HIS BACK AND LIES NEXT TO a younger man he barely knows.

"Should I go?" the mere acquaintance asks.

"No. Stay. I mean, if you want to."

So they remain there on the bed, both staring uncomfortably at the ceiling, listening to the neighborhood clatter on the backside of Court Street. Johnny knows it was wrong to bring him here to this bed on the night of Yago's funeral, but what did it matter now? Who would care?

"I'm gonna go check on my kid. You want anything?" Johnny asks politely.

"Maybe a glass of water."

Johnny throws on his robe, a gift from Yago, purchased on Johnny's credit card. A black velvety affair with silver piping around collar and cuff that made Johnny feel like a lounge singer.

He finds Angelo sleeping on the rug next to his twin bed. The bed-side lamp is still on. Johnny gathers his son up and tucks him in properly. On the opposite side of the bed, he sees a pile of torn-up comic books. "Well, wee man, that's a better expression of grief than what I came up with."

Johnny is surprised to see that Allyssa is not only still at the apartment, but that she's in the kitchen with every light on. She is making, judging by the ingredients littering the countertops and table, oatmeal cookies, a favorite of the deceased. It's ten at night.

She looks back at him long and hard. There is flour in her curls and she looks a little like his Italian grandmother when she was interrupted with some silliness. Raisins are scattered on the floor.

"I'm not judging *you,*" is all she says as she returns to her baking.

"Nor I you. Fair enough? Anyway, it's just Bob."

Bob is code for "just a fuck." Yago coined it but both Allyssa and, just once, Johnny have used it to describe less-than-serious liaisons. Allyssa did date an NYU student named Bob for almost a year, but they all referred to him as Robert.

"Are any of the memorial cookies ready for burial in my belly?" Johnny asks.

"I burnt the first batch, got distracted by the radio," she admits. "It was still tuned into his hideous station and I was imagining him dancing like a nut job all around the kitchen. The second batch has about five minutes to go."

"I'll wait. Is there any milk?" He leans against the door frame.

She opens the refrigerator, pulls out the carton of milk, does a quick sniff check. "We'll get through this, Johnny, no matter how many cookies or Bobs it takes. We have to at least seem alright. For Angelo."

"Allyssa, Brooklyn's own St. Joan," Johnny says without much feeling. "You know I met him when I was 19 years old. He was 18. And not in the backroom of some bar but in a coffee shop on Seventh

Avenue. I worked there at the counter until two in the morning. I saw plenty, believe you me."

She's heard this more than once, and opens the oven door. "Nope, not yet."

"Yago would often appear about one, and not always completely sober. Never said much at first. Just sat there at the counter with his *cafe coco*, half coffee, half hot chocolate. His own concoction. I remember thinking, how perfect for the half man, half boy he was. He looked older than his years but came across to me as a little lost boy."

Johnny sits at the kitchen table and rubs his eyes with his fingertips. "A little lost boy with no job, no interest in more school, harboring a virus that had already killed so many. He started hanging out in the bars when he was 16! Abe at least got that right." He pauses and his head hangs almost to his chest.

"The lost boy became a lost man, but you know what, Allyssa B. Cakes? He never left me. I gave him the freedom to run but he never ran away. Do you know what song he would sing to me? You'll never believe this. "If it takes forever I will..." He now notices that Allyssa has left the room and he hears the whimpering of his son in the back bedroom.

"I love that song." It's Bob, clueless, in his briefs. "Hey, I'm gonna take off."

"Yeah, sure. Might want to throw on a coat."

After Bob grabs his things and scurries off, Johnny takes the cookies from the oven, shovels things into the sink, and prepares cookies and milk for three.

Angelo is still crying softly in Allyssa's arms. "Look what I've got!" Johnny places the tray on the bedstand and climbs in with them. "How about a road trip tomorrow afternoon? Kindergarten be damned! I feel like a sleepover at Papa's beach house."

"Will Papa be there?"

"No. We talked about that, remember? We won't be seeing Papa anymore."

"Because he's an angel?" Angelo asks hopefully.

Allyssa fires Johnny a look. *Is this our story?*

"Yes, because he's our special angel who will always, always be looking after us all."

Out of Angelo's eyeshot, Allyssa sticks her finger down her throat and then says, "Oh my God! Angels everywhere and there's even a troll under the bed." The boy is happily distracted and curls his body over the edge of the bed to check. "I don't see any troll."

"Bad Allyssa," Johnny says. "Bad, bad pagan Allyssa."

"Pay gun Allyssa! Afraid of trolls!" Angelo sings.

"Enough, little man. Let's eat these cookies and then cuddle up in the crumbs. Tomorrow we'll set up the restaurant and then take an afternoon drive. We can even leave some cookies out for Papa."

"Don't forget Santa," Allyssa whispers to Johnny and then to Angelo, "I hear that somebody you like a lot is going to be out there. But we'll leave that for a surprise."

Soon they all stretch out on the narrow bed, making Angelo the little snack in the middle. Johnny switches off the light, strokes his son's hair.

"Oven's off?" the baker asks.

"Yup. Sweet dreams, you little cookie monsters." His arm stretches across to Allyssa and he pushes her hair from her face, feels the silky wetness on her cheek, and knows that she, too, has lost a great deal.

‡ ‡ ‡

It isn't the uncomfortably small space he's allocated or a bizarre dream or even remorse that wakes Johnny, but his old pal, anger. His mind is spinning. *A heart attack, really?* Someone in a wrinkled white coat had delivered the news, pulled him aside in the waiting area. Johnny can't remember the name on the doctor's plastic tag. *Was he even a doctor? Why no autopsy? What was written on those papers he signed when his eyes were blinded with tears?*

He thinks back to one of the many appointments with doctors he and Yago had sat through. Yago never spoke, never asked a single question. All so hopeful, those early promising strategies, the anti-retroviral cocktails, the hit-hard, hit-early defense that had kept Yago reasonably healthy. But Johnny now remembers that one appointment where the shadow of risk of liver problems and myocardial infarction related to drug toxicity briefly hung over the conversation between the doctor and Johnny. Yago had been in treatment for what, 10 or 12 years at that time? But Yago shook his head *no!* Johnny said they would stick with what works. *A mistake? His mistake?*

Where had Yago been last Wednesday night? Who was he with? Was it just a harmless trick? Johnny thinks not.

He leaves the bed, adjusts the covers, and kisses them both.

Then Johnny sits at the kitchen table, and while he draws small circles in the flour and sugar on its surface, he tries to remember details from the last time he saw Yago. He had presented him with a plate of pasta with clams piled high on top, bread, a glass of Malbec. The restaurant was surprisingly busy on that Ash Wednesday, but the table tucked next to the kitchen door was the family table and that is where Yago sat. Johnny would often sit with him for a few minutes when he could, but this night was busy. This or something much like it had happened hundreds of times. Johnny can't recall any of the mundane conversation from their brief exchanges that night. Yago was simply eating and he himself was working. He does remember there was a book, a black book on the table next to the bowl of clam shells, which struck Johnny as odd. Yago was no reader; he preferred television or radio to fill empty time.

Now at the kitchen table, he reconstructs Yago as he stood to leave. He wore a tight-fitting black suit with narrow lapels, not the current style but probably something he found at a thrift store. Still, it fit him well, and was set off by the crisp white shirt he wore beneath it, buttoned up to the collar like a European. His long hair flowed over the collar, and for the first time, there in the soft yellow light of the bistro, Johnny saw a few strands of silver twirling through his curls. This with his stylishly unshaven face gave him an exotic, maybe more Greek than Latin look.

Oh yes, as Yago turned to leave, Angelo had bolted from the kitchen and ran to him. Yago raised him high above his head, and as he lowered him, the boy had asked if Yago was going to church. You know, with the suit and all. Yago said nothing but laughed as Angelo took the bright red fleece scarf he was wearing and draped it around Yago's neck. "It's cold at church," he had warned. Of course, Yago rarely went with them to church, wouldn't know that the basement Sunday school classroom was cold and damp.

When Yago went out, it was usually at night, sometimes to bartend. Sometimes not. But over the many years they'd been together and especially since Angelo was with them, Yago almost always came home. But not that night.

Johnny stands. He tries to remember if he kissed Yago before he left that evening. Probably. He hopes he did.

He writes a brief note to Allyssa, should she wake in the night. He then dresses and heads into the midwinter haze. It's Saturday, only 11 o'clock. People will just be going out. He waits 20 minutes at their station for the F train. Johnny rides to West 4th Street in the Village. There are questions he must ask, things he couldn't have asked at Turkuaz. Questions he didn't even have then. Yago had a favorite haunt; he will go there.

‡ ‡ ‡

Johnny can feel the throbbing bass from the music before he even opens the heavy wooden door. The one window is covered with wood planking on the inside and a few men stand outside smoking. What comfort Yago found in a place like this escapes Johnny.

Inside the lighting is even dimmer than the street, except for flashing lights that come from a backroom, popping like paparazzi shooting cameras at starlets. There's a long bar and plenty of empty stools. Johnny orders a beer and heads for the back. The noise there, the pounding, unrelenting sound seems to reset his heartbeat to its pulsing rhythm. Before him bob all sorts of manhood, some shirtless, some shouting lyrics. Quite a few rim the room with drinks in hand and backs against walls. In the darkness with only flashes of light, it reminds him of driving through the Midtown Tunnel. For some unknown reason, he thinks of epileptics and the danger inherent in them being either in that tunnel or here, as if either could induce seizure. The scene is at once both familiar and foreign to him. He long ago lost the need or desire for a bar such as this.

But he is not here to dance or hustle or drink. Johnny leaves his beer on a narrow shelf and dives into the crowd, dancing in a way that Yago found laughable. Everyone saw Yago as a great dancer; his body moved as if in water, fluid and graceful. Johnny was more like a misfiring piston, his movements random and unrelated. Only when he was in Yago's arms could his own body respond to the music in a rhythmic pattern.

The first person he recognizes is actually a friend of both of theirs. Johnny had to shout his questions to him, but the man was unable to tell him anything about Yago on his last night. Hadn't seen him out and about. Hadn't heard anything about him. Was sorry, but "Hey, that was a some send-off at the restaurant. Yago would have had a great time." *Okay, not a particularly close friend.*

Back into the crowd, like diving for treasure in a vast, indifferent ocean, goes Johnny again and again. He shouts his discomforting questions at strangers, acquaintances, guys he's served at his restaurant. Almost everybody knows Yago, but no one has answers, until he spies Bob in the bouncing crowd and asks him. "Why didn't you ask me earlier," Bob says. "I thought you knew who he was seeing."

And what Mr. Justafuck reveals is something Yago never would have told Johnny and something Johnny never would have guessed.

CHAPTER NINE • ALIZARIN CRIMSON

The Fourth Day After Ash Wednesday

AS THE SKY SHIFTS FROM A DAWN OF FORMLESS WHITE TO a soft, clear blue—which no one is awake to witness—chunks of snow sporadically fly from limbs to ground. Whereas the city might be merely cool and wet, here in the tiny hamlet of Orient still throbs the cold heart of winter.

The water is calm beyond the collar of icy snow at the high tide mark. There are lanky cedars and pines that lurk around the small house. Small shrubs buried in new snow, tight little mounds looking like adolescent breasts, scatter the near landscape.

Sarah sits on a wooden stool at the kitchen counter, mesmerized by the images beyond the two large north-facing windows. The room is awash in clear light, saturating the pale face of the man at the sink. She is accustomed to the firm lines of urban architecture, comfortable with rounded curbs and the sharp edges of the shadows of tall buildings. Everything here is free verse, flowing, in constant motion—the evergreen limbs, gentle waves, snow bits descending in an almost horizontal fashion. Piano, she thinks a Chopin nocturne, drifts into the kitchen from a radio in another room. It is a lovely melody but sounds so melancholy and turgid in this strange, austere setting.

He beats eggs, melts butter in a cast iron skillet, grates cheese, and then pours more coffee into her mug.

"I am so comfortable with you," he tells her. "Feels like we've been together a long time."

"You're good at this," she says.

"No," Darby says, "I mean it. Yesterday was a horrible day and being with you is the only thing that got me through it."

"Darby, we need to have a real conversation. A couple of people at the restaurant asked how long we'd been together. I said not long, thinking less than 24 hours might seem inappropriate given the circumstances. Is there a bus or train that I can take back to the city?"

"No, I mean, of course there is. Please stay. At least have breakfast."

He piles the eggs and two slices of toast unattractively on a plate for her, places a fork in her hand. She is suddenly ravenous and begins eating before he serves himself. She eats in silence, as Darby stands behind her, stroking the nape of her neck.

"I love the city. It feeds my energy, my passion, my art. But this place, this is where I swam with my son, slept with Alejandra in the same bed, not like in the city where we both slept in random places at random times. Here we made love and mayhem, in this magically beautiful place. Looked more like real parents. There were many painters and writers and poets out here. We had friends. Parties."

"Where is this elusive Alejandra? Why wasn't she there yesterday?"

"Oh, Alejandra comes as Alejandra goes, whimsically and without warning. I assume she knows what happened but I didn't call her. Last I heard, she was in LA. She might even be back in Costa Rica for all I know."

He drags his fingers down her spine, rests his hands on her hips. "The vast blue of this sky here is not the fragmented blue of the Tribeca sky. The greens in Washington Square are muted and not these electric greens. Snow here is lighter, whiter, and more animated. Of course, it's the light. I rarely paint here. The honesty of the light betrays me."

Sarah stands and turns towards him. "At last, some truth."

The walls are white. The cupboards are white. Her empty plate is messy but white. Even the wooden floor beneath her is white-washed. Adorned in his white chamois shirt, she turns to him and mingles her black hands with his white hair. She craves a world this simple…black and white. What is right clearly separated from what is sinful, what is love from what is merely lust. But this is not the world she lives in and she wonders what right she has to judge, really, either William or Bennetta?

"I've run away from my life," Sarah says flatly.

"I know. Take mine."

It is at once the saddest, most pretentious, and yet the most painfully romantic thing ever said to her. His breakfast will grow cold.

Sarah takes his hand and they tackle the noisy old stairs to the second floor and back into his bedroom. The bed seems much too small for him, let alone for another large adult. She sits him there, removes his shirt, leans down and kisses him. And then in a more deliberate and sober way, this woman and her deflated artist come together and playfully make love, or play love. No questions this time, only a teasing exploration of bodies accompanied by melodic moaning. Then as she holds the headboard to counter his thrusts inside her, the bed gives way, one rail completely ripping from the footboard. This puts them at an uphill angle, but does not deter their efforts to complete the task at hand. She wraps her legs around him and once they both are satisfied, they slide pillow, woman, and man to the floor.

This is cause for laughter and more distraction from the tension in their lives. He pulls the blankets from the bed, wraps them both up and they sleep there on the rug for an hour or so.

Once awake, Sarah lifts Darby's arm from her waist and moves slowly to all fours. Using the broken bed as support, she carefully brings her aching body erect. She acknowledges that perhaps this was one more bit of unwise impulsivity, not the sex, but sleeping on the floor for even this short a time. She stretches and twists her naked body to ease the painful stiffness, then puts on his shirt and the sweatpants that Darby had pulled earlier from a box in the closet. They obviously were not his sweatpants as they only went midcalf on Sarah, necessitating the thinning wool socks he also had provided.

Darby begins to stir and eventually rolls to his side. "I'm going to need some help," he admits.

On the first floor of the house at the base of the stairs is a large room that at one time was likely two. It is a jumble of worn furniture including chairs which look like porch furniture, but sporting grand, colorful pillows. Sarah has never been in a beach house such as this. She finds a book and her way to the oversized couch. Darby puts on another pot of coffee and turns the radio from the sleepy classical to a more upbeat jazz station.

"Sarah, stay awhile before you return to the life you've run away from," he says and sits on the opposite end of the couch. "We all do things to enable us to forget other things. I would never judge you. I'll take you to our favorite place for dinner and I promise, in the morning, to drive you back to Manhattan."

She doesn't reply but smiles sweetly, almost maternally, at him and tightens into a smaller ball on the couch. "I love this poet," she does say and returns to her book.

Darby was not aware that this book of poetry was in the house. He sees on the cover the name of the poet, Neruda. Alejandra's.

"Read one to me," Darby says. "I'd much rather be read to than to read myself."

Clouds now fill the sky as the temperature drops further.

Sarah reads this to him:

> Being *never was once: we went on being. Other feet,*
> *other hands, other eyes.*
> *All things in their passing kept changing, like leaf after leaf*
> *on a tree. And in you? Your skin changed,*
> *your hair and your memory: you were never that other.*
> *That was a child loping by at a run,*
> *a boy on a bicycle on the opposite side of the river,*
> *in whose motion*
> *your whole life passed by in the stress of a moment.*

"Read it again."

She does.

"What follows that?"

Sarah reads ahead and continues with these lines:

> *The child's mask kept changing,*
> *his mournful occasions subsided,*
> *he steadied his altering mastery:*
> *his skeleton toughened,*
> *the device of his bones was accomplished,*
> *his smile,*
> *his manner of walking*

She stops midway through the line. Pauses. He has inched closer on the couch.

"I could read another one to you," Sarah says.

"Please, go on."

She skims ahead a little; he wouldn't notice. She reads:

> *all kept on happening*
> *one man impurely persisting,*
> *son of the purely born son,*

till nothing remained as it was.
Little by little, the face of a stranger
looked out of my face—
though my face remained changelessly there.

There is more, but she stops. There is much buried in these beautiful words, but she knows they are a painful collection of words for him.

"I don't know exactly what the poet means, but this poem does make me think of Yago," Darby says finally. "I would see his face in mine when I looked into the mirror after I'd been painting him for hours, for days. I've had many exhibitions of portraits only of him. I don't think he even once went to any of them. Please read those last lines one more time, beginning with 'little by little.'"

Sarah obliges.

"And what's the name of this poem?" asks Darby.

"'El Niño Perdido.' 'Little Boy Lost.' I'm sorry, really sorry."

More long minutes pass. Darby puts his face into his hands. "Did I become a stranger to myself?" he asks, looking back at her. "I surely grew to be a stranger to him. Now I find I have lost him. A whole piece of myself, of my past, goes with him."

A lone saxophone weeps from the radio in such a melodramatic way that Darby's heartfelt words seem like a movie moment. He shakes his head. "Coffee?"

After serving his guest, Darby eats his cold eggs, washed down with hot coffee. The kitchen stool beneath him had been Yago's perch while he watched his mother make magic with odd little chile pods and unmarked jars of spice. He walks to the cabinet where there are still many jars such as that, the ancient dried chiles, and a bottle of vanilla from Mexico that has no liquid in it, only sepia stains on the plastic. He finds an IGA plastic bag and drops into it all the items on that shelf, along with the memories attached to them. He ties a couple of sturdy knots and places the bag by the back door.

When he returns to the front room with arms full of logs, Sarah has barely touched her coffee and continues to read the book of poems. He makes a fire in the woodstove but leaves the door open with a screen in place. The sounds of the growing, snapping fire add a subtle syncopation to the percussion of the now Latin music from the radio. Darby's mood lightens or his attention shifts adequately enough for him to ask, "May I paint you?"

"Paint me? Why?" Not a vain woman, Sarah still knows the toll paid for her advanced years and for the chaotic weekend thus far. She hasn't even washed her face and her only makeup is the tube of lipstick from her coat pocket.

"I could lie and say that it would be therapeutic for me, and maybe it would be," Darby tells her. "I don't know why, but I want to. Maybe to know you better."

Since she doesn't immediately refuse, he sets up the easel, canvas, brushes and oils, all stored in what would be logically a coat closet by the front door. He places the kitchen stool near the woodstove and fetches a white flannel sheet from the broken bed. He then takes her book and marks her place with a matchbook. He pulls her to her feet and with the detachment of a family physician, removes her clothing while keeping his eyes locked on hers. Darby wraps her in the sheet.

Sarah walks to the stool. "You have 30 minutes."

He takes her by the shoulders and attempts to position her on the stool, but Sarah pushes the artist's hands away. She squares her shoulders and spreads her legs slightly with her feet wrapped around the stool's legs. "I don't need the sheet, unless you do," she says, and lets it fall to rest on her forearms, exposing her long neck and low, full breasts, rounded abdomen, and a shock of grey pubic hair against her rich brown skin.

"I don't think it's fair, however, that I am naked and you are clothed," she announces.

"You're kidding."

"Not at all. I would be so much more relaxed if you removed *your* clothes for me."

The *for me* intrigues him so he obliges, removing his sweater and then his undershirt. There is nothing beneath his trousers, so he hesitates. "Everything?"

"You can keep your socks. The floors are cold."

So he lets his trousers fall to the floor and kicks them away. "Let's pretend we are the last two people on earth. Adam and Eve come full circle."

"Born of heaven. Destined for?" she adds.

"I don't believe in hell."

"Neither do I anymore," Sarah says. "So paint."

Darby sidesteps his way to his canvas, worrying that his backside might be less than flattering. "Turn your head away from me just a little. Look towards the window there. Sarah, you have my complete attention."

She smiles at his old world egotism as she takes her last glance at the flaccid genitalia that will be hidden by his canvas. "Yes, give me your complete attention," she says, crossing her arms below her breasts as she turns away from him.

There's that defiant Orient light confronting him. He watches closely as it falls upon her, diffused, yet so honest, animated, even mystical. If only he could capture that in paint, the light itself, which he knows is impossible, because it always shifts, takes on new personalities. There are tricks with paints which can be used to capture and portray light...velvety titanium white with its high reflectance, transparent yellows and oranges, and metallic paints with tiny flecks of bronze or aluminum powder. Light has to fall on objects to be recorded. Pure light, even light on molecules in the air, is abstract and best left, in his opinion, to abstract painters, which he is not.

"Twenty-seven minutes remaining," she estimates.

Abraham Darby feels vulnerable and suddenly inept. The diffused blanket of light that separates him from his subject is intimidating and she seems more the one in control. "I need my trousers," he admits nervously. "I can't paint like this."

"Really?" She pulls the sheet up around her.

"No! Don't do that. Let me try."

She pulls away her sheet, but then he hides his vulnerability with a cowardly lowering of the easel bed.

"That's cheating and you know it, Mr. Darby."

"I'm quite shy."

"Nonsense. I won't even be looking at you. Raise your canvas again and I'll drop the sheet completely."

"You'll be cold."

"You'll add wood to the fire," she says.

And so the canvas height is adjusted and Sarah Obadias lets the sheet cascade to the floor. "Do I look like a roasted turkey on a white Thanksgiving tablecloth?"

"You look good to me," Darby tells her. "Good enough to eat."

She focuses on a lovely watercolor hanging between the windows that she had not noticed before. It depicts a young boy, an almost translucent figure with wet hair obscuring most of his face, except for his full-lipped and sensuous mouth. He seems at once to frolic in and yet float above the aqua water. There are spongy green hills in the distance and shining purple sand drifts in the foreground.

She knows that this surely can't be Orient and this isn't a work of Darby's.

Thick lines of dioxazine purple, Van Dyke brown, yellow ochre, and naphthol scarlet are applied to Darby's crude palette, which is merely a common composite container usually found beneath raw meat. Then bold lines of bone black, raw sienna, titanium white, and a metallic copper are added. Darby takes his Double Thick Filbert, blends several colors, and examines the woman on the stool before him.

When he begins to apply paint to the oil-primed canvas, it is on her face that he concentrates his initial efforts. He renders the delicate line from her nostril to the corner of her lip and the seductive curves of her half-opened eyes, then her high-priestess forehead, long neck and sharp dissecting collarbones. Her breasts are painted with his fingertips. The shadows of her face are purply black and the high-lighted planes of her upper torso become the color of cream stirred into coffee.

More than 27 minutes pass. Wood is added to the stove.

Without manipulation, the music shifts to a classical piece, introduced as Bach's Suite No. 1 for Lute and by the lovely name Bourrée. Sarah finds it crisp, calming, perfect music for winter, with the clean tripping of notes, bouncing off the white of the canvas's edges and Darby's snowy hair.

He doesn't notice her occasional glances at him or even that the music has changed so dramatically. All he needs is sound enough to drown out the pounding silence in his head and time enough to paint.

Sarah knows little about his style of painting, the level of abstraction he dares, or what formal training he has undertaken. The portraits in his loft she remembers as beautifully executed but emotionally distant, perhaps because the subject rarely looked at the artist directly. Or so she recalls. *Why couldn't she look at him?* Is it the light he seeks to control or his own distance? A huge portrait who she knows now is his son had leaned against a wall in what was loosely his kitchen area. The figure was frozen in time sitting at a table in conversation, turned away from the viewer, and the artist. His leg was outstretched behind him and he was leaning towards his unseen companion. The room was very dark in the painting but the figure of the young man was bathed in a golden light, as if shining from above. She had liked the painting but couldn't grasp its meaning or relevance.

She thinks about one more painting, this one at the funeral party at Turkuaz. It was a tall, slim canvas of a standing, shirtless Yago, hands shoved deep into his jean's pockets, his shoulders narrow, belly with a subtle paunch, a hairless chest. His head was hanging a bit but his eyes were locked with hers in a yearning, almost angry glare. It felt like the artist had taken him apart cell by cell, and then reconstructed him stroke by stroke on his canvas. All the rich hues utilized in depicting his golden skin and faded blue jeans composed the abstracted background as well, making the young man seem to float in a sea of lush but muted colors. Heavy black lines and shading outlined the figure's form and features, which suggested the initial sketch.

While elsewhere Darby's paint was thick but flat, viewed from a short distance, this larger-than-life portrait was alarmingly realistic, as though Yago was striking a pose there next to the hummus and skewered lamb, both pulling her towards him while simultaneously rejecting her.

Before she had left the restaurant, she approached the work once more, needing more time to understand both subject and artist. No authorization was required from the subject to get closer. From that intimate distance, she had witnessed the complex blending of paint that she knew was the beauty of working in oils. A small tent card placed on a table nearby had informed her that Abraham Darby's painting of Yago was only visiting—he was on loan from the Manning Gallery, New York, New York.

Now naked in the presence of the great painter—who has like a thief retrieved his trousers—she thinks she should feel honored that he has chosen her, for his bed and his canvas. Perhaps she is, but she also feels anxious. *What would become of this portrait?* Would this possession of his be recognizable as Sarah Obadias and would it ever hang at this Manning Gallery...or in Atlanta where her daughter lives?

As the midafternoon light slices through clouds, a sharp wind rattles the house and swings wide open the kitchen's back door. But it isn't just the power of the wind, as there, visible only to Sarah, stands a woman in a long, black coat with a scarf of brilliant oranges and bright greens wrapped around her neck and half of her face. Galaxies of swirling dark hair are piled on top of her head and her large, smiling eyes are lined with heavy black inking. She lowers a satchel and a brown paper bag to the kitchen floor and walks with hands on hips to the front room.

Sarah hops from her stool and wraps the sheet around her, holding it tight under her chin.

"Alejandra! Unannounced as usual," Darby says.

"I thought you might be here as you were not at the loft. This was always such a beautiful place to be sad," Alejandra says, and then to Sarah, "I've heard about you, Reverend Obadias. It is a pleasure to meet you. I am Alejandra Morales Díaz, the mother of Yago Darby Díaz." She walks to Sarah and extends her still gloved hand daintily.

"Reverend?" Darby is staring at the woman in the sheet. "You're a minister?"

"Nice to meet you," Sarah says, looking around the room. "I need to get dressed."

"No. No. This is a lovely thing for a winter afternoon following a funeral." She shoots a look at Darby. "I am the one who is dressed inappropriately."

"Stop staring, Darby. I told you we needed to talk," Sarah says.

"You're a minister?" he repeats. He gathers Sarah's clothes for her, but Alejandra takes them immediately from him.

"You must continue painting," Alejandra announces, walking back into the kitchen. "I brought some beautiful Rioja. I will join you." Her cell phone emits a muffled ringing from her satchel and she closes the French doors for privacy.

"Are you married as well? Commit any felonies?" His hair is in his eyes and his arms are thrust downward at his sides.

"I have nothing to explain to you, Darby. You haven't needed to know anything more about me than what music I listen to when I'm upset. Do you even remember my answer?"

"Nina Simone. And your favorite book was the Bible! *Ha!* Was that a clue?"

"And you asked if anyone was waiting for me at home."

"You said no one. But are you married?" He is flushed and sweating.

"Not really."

"Sarah, that is a question with a yes or a no answer."

She sits on her stool. "More no than yes. That's all I will say. And you? The *two of you* lived together, raised a son, vacationed here, made love in the same bed that we just fucked in, I bet. Were you married? Yes or no?"

"Biscotti?" an amused Alejandra asks as she returns with that and the wine and three stemless glasses. "We were never married. But the thing about the bed, that is true. But, please, let's be civil and sympathetic. It has already been too much, this weekend." She pours and serves. "To Yago, our beloved boy."

Sarah finds the toast unusual, from a minister's point of view, accustomed to praying for the dead, not toasting them. "Yes…to Yago.

My deepest sympathy to you both."

"Ha!" Darby says inexplicably. Alejandra feels like a shot of adrenaline into his grieving and everything is rushing to the surface. He knocks back the wine and then shoves the empty glass in her face. "Where the hell have you been?"

Alejandra fills his glass with the balance in the bottle. There is a tiny rivulet of tears beneath her left eye only. "Abraham, some kindness please. I was in Escazú. Why did you not call me? You have the number, all my numbers. Did you even try? I think *no*. Johnny called me only Friday. But what difference does that make? I have no desire to attend my son's funeral. I will say goodbye to him in my own way. And I am glad I was not there! I was told about your harsh words. Abraham, really?"

"It eats me alive! You must admit it, Alejandra. If he was not a homosexual, he would never have contracted AIDS."

"Stop this, Darby!" Sarah stands between them in her flowing white sheet, again the intervening angel.

"If you're going to tell me, Minister, about your loving and forgiving God, forget it. There's no proof of that," Darby mocks.

"Let him believe this. It is his right," Alejandra says. "We all have to make sense of his passing. To me, Yago died as if a soldier in war…"

Darby snorts a dismissive laugh, but she continues. "A war he did not choose to fight in. Abraham believes he did choose it. This is our difference. Yago battled this disease for many, many years. I really did think I would lose him long ago. But this cocktail kept him well enough, but it also weakened him.

"But no matter. He is gone and no day will pass that I will not cry for him."

No one has touched the biscotti but Alejandra fetches a second bottle of the Rioja. The music has become a wearing delivery of the troubling news of the world. Alejandra flips it off. "I'd rather listen to the wind."

Darby takes his glass and heads for the kitchen, muttering. "There are feelings and there are facts. I believe in facts." Before closing the doors between the two rooms, he adds, "And *that* is the difference between us."

Alejandra stokes the fire. "He loved his son, yes. But it was more like a son loves a father, you know, a love full of expectation and need."

Then Alejandra comes very close to Sarah. She is a much smaller woman but is eye to eye with her on her stool. Alejandra loosens Sarah's one-handed grip on the sheet at her neck and she opens the two halves enough to reveal only the space between her breasts. Then she takes the wineglass from Sarah's other hand and sips. "Just who are you and how is it you are with Darby here? Johnny is quite a fan of yours. We often like the same people. And the same people often like us."

Sarah remembers after a brief silence that there had been a question in all of that. "I'm just a friend…of Darby's."

"He has many friends."

"No doubt," says Sarah.

"Your name is lovely. Obadias. Where does that come from?"

"I wanted a name that was not a slave name. I did a lot of research and found this African name. It has the same meaning in Hebrew and Arabic."

"I see. And what does it mean, this new name of yours?"

"Servant. More specifically, servant of God."

"Isn't that perfect." Alejandra sits on the couch and pats the space next to her. Once Sarah is settled and her sheet is arranged appropriately around her, Alejandra continues. "I feel I make you uncomfortable."

"My life makes me uncomfortable."

"You are married?"

"Separated."

"And a practicing minister...with parishioners?"

"No longer."

"Retired?"

"No."

"You are a woman of short, enigmatic answers," Alejandra says. "*Enigma*, you know, it is the same word in English and in Spanish. But is this a good thing, a minister *misterioso*?"

"Darby and I met at a restaurant a couple nights ago," Sarah digresses. "I had no idea what was happening in his life."

"But you go to his son's funeral with him?"

"He didn't tell me where we were going. I didn't care."

"I see. A distraction." Alejandra goes to the coat closet and pulls out another canvas, the same medium-sized canvas as Darby's, and a small suitcase. "I prefer the acrylics. At least for New York. Watercolors are best for Escazú." A second easel appears and she sets up five or six feet from Darby's easel.

"My son had been dying for some time," she says, looking not at Sarah but at Darby's painting of her. "I don't mean dying of AIDS, but in his spirit. I would say that he was suffering from a malady of the soul. I don't know where it came from. I thought I saw it lift when Angelo came into his life, but it was temporary. I know he tried. I always made it a point to see my son whenever I was in New York. We spent time here in Orient, too; Darby is generous with his family's home. But Yago was struggling in many ways. For me, always the happy facade. A mother knows.

"This sadness in Yago was absent when he was a boy. You see that watercolor of him there? He was in the magical waters of the

Caribbean Sea, almost floating above them in his simple happiness, the glorious morning light illuminating him from within."

"Yes, I see that. I was admiring your work…"

"It seems he was born to be painted," Alejandra interrupts Sarah's reflexive compliment. "In Darby's portraits Yago is much heavier, buried in the thick oils. Of course, they are beautiful works, much in demand. I doubt that Darby knows that quite a few of his buyers are wealthy gay men. Isn't that ironic?" She again looks at his portrait of Sarah. "Darby paints from his gut, not so much from his heart. His work is alarmingly real. I don't mean realistic. But real in that they are mortal, sober portraits that convey a deep vulnerability in both subject and artist. They are often confrontational. As was his relationship with his son."

Alejandra begins to undress, removing her black sweater and then her brassiere. She is a younger woman than Sarah, only in her late fifties. "Forgive me. I go on and on. But if you ask me, and I know you have not, I would say that Yago was homosexual because he was looking always to find himself. Not scientific, I know, and not politically correct. But he was my son, and this is what I saw in him."

Sarah looks out a window and then to the floor. When she dares to look at Alejandra again, she sees that she has placed the canvas against the back of a chair and has hoisted her skirt, and now straddles the chair facing the blank canvas. Then, even more baffling to Sarah, Alejandra squeezes a large curl of reddish orange paint into her right palm, then rubs the paint in a large band around the nipples of her small breasts.

"Nowhere is it written that only a brush is allowed to touch the canvas," she informs Sarah as she pulls the stretched linen to her chest. "There, a good start. But I will need more paint to do justice to your lovely bosom. Please drop your sheet and let us see who captures more of the minister—her lover or her competition."

Darby has been watching them through the French doors. He now opens them and announces his willingness to participate. "But be careful, Sarah, because it's you we're competing for."

Sarah feels like a character in a work of fiction, fiction of the type she would never read. She decides to play along and leaves her stool once more. She strolls over to the plate of biscotti, snatches two and returns to her perch. She lowers the sheet only to her lap. "Have fun then, you two, but I want a proper meal once you are finished with your works of art."

"May I suggest the Lookout Pub," Alejandra says, and she takes the canvas to her easel and begins to paint.

"We agree," Darby adds. "For once."

A shock of late afternoon sun with the color and effervescence of champagne infuses the room. The two topless painters become lost in their work, which is now a moving subject as Sarah nibbles on her biscotti. She can actually hear the brushstrokes falling on canvas. The quiet in the room is broken only by that and the wind rattling the old windowpanes.

Darby is more aggressive in the way he attacks his canvas, as though two sides of his personality are battling. He sometimes shakes his head or runs his hand through his hair. Often there is a look of puzzlement, followed by more energetic application of paint. His eyes dart from painting to subject, while Alejandra focuses on Sarah for minutes at a time, then closes her eyes before bringing her brush to the canvas. Her strokes are long and fluid.

Shortly after five in the afternoon on the far eastern end of Long Island, evening arrives. The room gradually slips into near darkness with only the fire in the stove offering weak illumination for the final work. Then the session ends and Sarah is offered first dibs on the shower. But before she climbs to the second floor to prepare herself for the Lookout Pub, she asks to see the paintings, but is denied.

"They must cure," Darby tells her. "Let us find some fresh clothes for you."

‡ ‡ ‡

Sarah has finished in the bathroom and there on the broken bed is a mix of men's and women's clothing to choose from. Of course, Darby's shirts and sweaters are much too large and Alejandra's too small. She has no desire to wear again her outfit from Friday night. Even in its rumpled state, it feels too formal. Her underpants are missing, but she cannot bring herself to put on another woman's pair so she goes without. She pulls on black leggings that only reach her midcalf and the wool socks that will be hidden by her tall boots. She selects a black cotton turtleneck that must be Darby's and a long grey vest of Alejandra's. She ties around her neck the horrid plaid scarf Darby purchased on the street for her only yesterday, and then examines the effect of it all in a floor-length mirror on the closet door.

The woman reflected there is not her as she knows herself, but a woman on the run, morphing into another version of herself. The outfit is laughable but appropriate enough. With the addition of a little moisturizer and the eye makeup Alejandra also has placed on the bed, she is comfortable enough to be seen in public.

At this same time, Alejandra is in the shower washing the acrylic paint from her chest. Darby is shaving at the sink. "How often has this happened," he asks as he pulls back the shower curtain a bit, "that you show up as I begin a relationship?"

"Close the curtain!" she shouts.

"Why, Tica? You were half naked downstairs. Anyways, I've seen every inch of you."

She yanks the curtain closed. "Not in a blessed long time. And every time I do show up, you are with a new woman."

"I haven't been with anyone for years."

"Only me," she counters, "and it was for only five years."

"That's not what I meant, Alejandra."

"Yes, I know. Can shampoo go bad? This smells dreadful."

"It's been many years since I slept with any woman. You may have been the last. Remember LA?"

"Oh God, Abraham! Must we go there?" But she adds as she rinses her hair, "We are no better at breaking up than being together."

Minutes later, she turns off the water and steps naked from the tub. "A towel please."

"You are one confusing woman," Darby says.

"So what was it...you just could not resist a preacher?"

"You know I didn't know that. I was at Malatesta with Johnny and a couple of his annoying friends. I didn't know the other men at all and I think Johnny invited them for cover. We ate, drank too much wine, and talked about him...and the funeral and burial arrangements. I had little to say and couldn't wait to get away from them."

Alejandra is slipping into her dress, the same black dress that Sarah wore to her son's funeral. Length and fit are perfect but she sees a streak of clumpy whitish something just below the graceful neckline. She wets a corner of her towel and blots away what is likely a remnant from Turkuaz. "Did she wear this to my son's funeral? This is what you gave to her to wear? Why didn't you call me when it happened? Why is it almost two days past before I learn of his death?"

Darby stops buttoning his shirt and sits on the lid of the toilet. "I only learned about it on Thursday night. Johnny phoned me, said that Yago had suffered a heart attack. Couldn't be revived. He was already at the funeral home in Brooklyn. *Imagine that.* Like I, too, was an afterthought. I went there immediately and saw what was left of our son. There was heavy makeup on his face but I could still see the bruises. I saw Johnny with his friends, laughing, like they're at a party, for God's sake. There was our Yago laid out like a comedian in an awful suit and bow tie. Was that supposed to be funny? He would not have wanted that."

Yago's mother leans heavily against the bathroom door. She wants him to stop with this, but she needs to know everything there is to tell. "I heard from Johnny that he was bruised from his fall. I am blessed to remember him as I last saw him. But the tie, Abraham, was it red?"

"I don't know," Darby says angrily. "Maybe. No, it *was* red."

"I gave him that tie. It's a very expensive one. He always wore it for me when we would go to a nice restaurant. There are so many things you don't know about your son."

"That's not my fault!"

"It doesn't matter now," she says. "Please. Tell me everything."

"There isn't much more to tell. I walked away from the casket and went to leave. I was too angry to cry. Johnny came running over to me, dragging the boy with him. I didn't want to talk to him. I mean, a day after the fact, he *phones* me to tell me my son is dead. I asked him why Yago was bruised. He just said he'd come by and talk to me in the morning, tell me everything he knew, which wasn't much. And he said he wanted paintings of Yago for the funeral.

"I felt as out of his life as always. I was fuming. I told him to take whatever he wanted. That's what he'd already done, wasn't it?"

"So why did you meet him at Malatesta?" She checks her watch and thinks she may have made a serious mistake.

"I drank that night, home, alone. I thought about calling you but I knew I couldn't say those words to you. I slept late on Friday, not well, but late. He was buzzing me from downstairs. I felt numb, which was a blessing. I didn't feel like fighting. I picked out a few paintings and then we drove over to the gallery and borrowed one from their collection. He told me that he'd called you. He asked me to have dinner with him, so we could talk about the funeral. Told me I could speak at the funeral, if I wanted to."

"We should go soon," she interrupts.

"I knew she was watching me from the bar. When I sat next to her I could feel she needed me, too. Or so I thought. I really don't know what either of us was looking for, but I knew the alcohol wasn't doing the job."

"Very romantic, but enough. I know you well enough to know the rest." And she leaves the bathroom.

‡ ‡ ‡

Alejandra finds Sarah standing in the front room, staring at the two canvases. She has placed them on a bed of old magazines on the couch. The lampshade is off the lamp on the coffee table.

"This light is very unflattering, but what do you think? Who captured you the best?" Alejandra asks.

There is no way any observer would know the paintings are of the same person. Darby's does resemble Sarah, but a reconstructed, somewhat romanticized version. Individual planes of thick, richly hued strokes of paint render her skin supple and sensuous. There are also delicate lines of color that connect elements of the face or underscore the fullness of her lower lip. Her eyes are closing, sexy and knowing. She looks on the verge of orgasm and Sarah feels he has revealed too much.

Blacks are tinted with blues and browns with reds. Everything above and to the sides of her head is lost in abstracted shadow, and below the deep curves of her breasts is the formless sheet like a bed of clouds. He has not painted away her age, but only played with it, splashing in her past like a child in a puddle.

Sarah feels exposed, as if he has made love to her in paint. It's a skilled and intimate work and she feels something in her gut sink.

"As I told you, he is very good. He will sell this for a lot of money," Alejandra says flatly. "But look at mine. Take time and then tell me what you see."

In terms of palette, it is opposite. Sarah is bathed in vibrant reds and oranges and even the blacks have heat in them. It's not anything like the pose Sarah had held there on the stool. Her dark arms are crossed beneath the imprint of Alejandra's breasts and her head tilts back, as if in laughter or defiance, creating a long, lovely neck. Again, an accomplished work, but in addition to the fiery eroticism there is one other thing that jars Sarah.

"My face," she tells the artist. "It's white."

"Yes. I was not painting your skin."

CHAPTER TEN • SHATTERED BEER BOTTLE GREEN

NOBODY BREAKS THE DENSE SILENCE DURING THE DRIVE TO Greenport with Darby at the wheel. At the end of Main Street, he takes a hard left down into an alleyway. Two short blocks further and they arrive at the Lookout Pub and away from the more upscale establishments that have better views of the harbor.

Sarah had sat next to Darby on the ride over, her thigh touching his. He had seemed sullen and lost in his thoughts, but all she could think about was his painting of her. Something about it needed reconciling with the space she protectively, but perhaps wrongly, put between them. He has exposed something powerful in her and this painting has rendered her both uncomfortable and intrigued.

Alejandra, meanwhile, had stared out the window the entire trip.

The parking lot is half full at exactly seven. "You go in," Alejandra directs them. "Get our table, Darby. I am going to smoke."

"I'll be at the bar," he says, taking off on his own.

"Then you must join me," Alejandra tells Sarah while extracting a cigar from her bag. She hands it to her companion. In the hazy lighting of the parking lot, Sarah can only make out an oval frame containing a hand with a leaf on the gold band. "From my country,"

Alejandra explains. "Vegas de Santiago. Tobacco touched by the gods. Not your God, of course, but the gods of nature." She takes the cigar back and performs the ritualistic mouthing of the thing, then lights up.

"Do you smoke? Maybe sometimes? You must try it."

Sarah finds herself accepting. She takes a small drag, exhales quickly, and passes it back.

Then through the harbor mist, an old Volvo station wagon pulls up next to them and out climb Johnny, Allyssa, and the boy.

"Oh, there you are!" Alejandra sings. "Perfect timing."

"Reverend, you persist, I'm happy to see." Johnny gives Sarah an awkward embrace. "But still not in your own clothes, I'm afraid."

"What a lovely surprise," Sarah says, and she means it. They look like a three-pack of lightness and levity. "And here's my new friend, Angelo."

But Angelo and Allyssa are scampering over to the main attraction, Alejandra, who hands the cigar to Johnny and takes them both into her arms. "Abuelita!" Angelo squeals as he buries his face into the folds of her coat.

Johnny stubs out the cigar on the gravel. "Disgusting habit for a man. Doubly grotesque on you, Mamacita. Every man who sees you with that thing in your mouth will think one thing."

"Who is hungry?" Alejandra chimes in, and then to Johnny, "Do *not* throw that thing away."

Angelo is fascinated by the vast collection of beer coasters that decorate the arched mudroom of the pub. Against the ochre walls, they are neatly arranged in rows and range from the obvious vintage Budweiser to the microbreweries, such as Back River, Greenport Harbor Brewery, and Neighbor's Dog Ale. Johnny holds him high so the boy can examine and touch the ones far above his head.

"I really am glad to see you," Sarah tells Johnny. "It's all been very strange."

"Welcome to my world," Johnny says. "Alejandra asked us to come out. She knew he'd be here, but thought there would be too many memories haunting him. It's gonna be weird for us all, without Yago, Mr. Let's-sleep-on-the-beach. Next to the Village, this was his favorite place in the world."

Once in the pub, Sarah looks left to the veritable altar to alcoholic spirits that stretches all the way to the back wall. The back bar is an oily, dark oak, with alcoves of stained glass, and a large central mirror in front of which are many bottles of booze. The stools are the swirling type you might find in a diner and on the second to the last is her date. His hands clutch a beer and there's an empty shot glass nearby.

"Johnny, take everybody to our table. I have reserved it for us," Alejandra says. "I will be right with you."

Past exposed brick and murky green wainscoting, the party travels to the rear of the dining room, which is separated from the bar area by a wall of open windows. Beneath the white, pressed-tin ceiling is their circular table with a perfect view of the workingman's harbor.

Back at the bar, Alejandra does not care for the man who is locked in an animated discussion with Darby. As she comes closer, she smells the engine oil on him, as well as the sad longing.

"What are you doing here?" she says rudely.

"He's our mascot," Zak, the Lookout's favorite bartender, says. She's wearing a beret, a flannel shirt, and a huge smile that is warm and authentic. "What can I getcha?"

"Hola Baby! Give me what Darby's drinking, minus the beer."

"You got it, Señora." Zak pours her a shot of Patrón. Darby points to the two empty shot glasses and she fills those as well.

Darby's sidekick stands and walks over to Alejandra. "He didn't tell me you were with him. He told me about Yago."

He looks like he's either going to belch or cry, she can't tell which, but she backs away. "Are you drinking, Zander? I thought that was one bad habit you gave up," Alejandra says. "That and me. Hey Zak, is he drinking?"

"Tonight he is."

Alejandra knocks back the shot. "We are waiting for you, Darby. I have our spot and a few surprises for you."

Back at the table, Angelo is trying to convince his father that french fries and Coke are a meal. Even though the hand-cut fries are served with English malt vinegar, Johnny's not impressed. "There's no real food in that. Throw in the vegetable egg rolls and you've got a deal."

Sarah is already ordering, "The haddock chowder. And right away, the beet salad, please. I'm famished. Oh, and a dry white wine, whatever you think is good."

"Beer for me, anything on tap and local," Johnny tells the waitress, a dishy blonde who happens to be Zak's girlfriend, Dee. Allyssa orders her predictable fish and chips and Johnny the Mumbai curry, but "please no tofu or chicken, just the shrimp."

Alejandra arrives and with an arm around Dee's waist, flirtatiously whispers to her, "Jack Daniels flank steak. Dos, por favor. And darling Dee, your favorite baked Jarlsberg for the table. Zak knows what I like for my wine."

By the time Darby shows up at the table, Sarah has finished both her salad and first glass of wine. The Jarlsberg and toasted ciabatta are history and the conversation centers on Yago.

"Every day his absence becomes more real, and not in a good way," Johnny is saying. He ignores Darby's noisy entrance, scraping his chair across the tile floor, sitting down heavily. "It's kind of like his absence is a new presence in my life, unavoidable, filling up space, making itself known always in new ways. I opened the door of his closet this morning, the smell of him everywhere. My brave Angelo threw out his toothbrush." He stops, looks at his son. "He told me angels don't get cavities."

Dee appears with steaming plates and a huge crock of chowder for Sarah. Darby immediately grabs his knife and fork and slices into his flank steak, even before all the others have been served. With his head hung low, he loads and reloads his fork, with only short breaks for beer consumption.

"Don't mind him," Alejandra explains to the table. "Abraham has only four avenues to vent pain—painting, drinking, eating, and well," now looking at Sarah, "you know the other."

"Johnny, please continue," Sarah says, although neither she nor anyone else wants him to go down that dark path again. She nods a thank you when a second glass of wine arrives, which she did not order.

"Life will never be normal," Johnny says, pulling Angelo's fingers from the deep recesses of his egg roll. "He was my normal."

Darby doesn't bother to look up from his plate, but mutters pejoratively, "Normal?"

"Yah, you know, Abe, my normal. You just strut over, sit, and shovel food into your mouth. You don't acknowledge me or Allyssa, or even Angelo. Must be your normal."

Allyssa pats Johnny's arm as if he were a dog. "He didn't mean anything. It's okay," she says to Darby.

"We had a normal life, Abe," Johnny says loudly to the top of Darby's head. "Normal! Bills, fights, infidelities! Just like you. Just like every fucking couple!"

Alejandra puts her hands over Angelo's ears. "Johnny, control yourself. The boy."

Darby looks up and glares at Johnny, which only fans the fire.

"Ear infections! Bed-wetting! Nightmares! Answering impossible questions!" Every word from Johnny's mouth a weapon, delivered not in high volume but high intensity, his eyes locked with Darby's until the widower looks away, adding, "But what would you know?"

Alejandra slams the butt of her steak knife against the tabletop like an angry queen. "Enough!" Other diners look, then look away. Angelo worms away from Allyssa and crawls under the table. Through a window in the partition, Sarah sees that the bartender and their waitress are conferencing. She senses a bigger scene is on its way.

"That's enough," Alejandra repeats. "The two of you! Is grief a competition? And normal? Why is this a goal?"

"I loved my son," Darby announces, a little too intoxicated at this point to answer Johnny's vague accusations, or even remember them.

"*I* loved your son." Johnny's lips quiver, whether from sadness or anger, no one is quite sure.

"Okay, we all agree. We all loved Yago. Do we need to scare his son under the table? Mind what you are teaching him." Alejandra raises her wineglass and looks to the tin ceiling. "I love you, too, my son, and I swear upon your grave that I will not allow your memory to be stained with such foolishness." Then, calmly and less dramatically, "Let's eat our meal like normal people, whoever that is."

And they do as directed, in silence, except for Johnny, who does not eat. He swirls his fork through his mild curry, pokes a shrimp occasionally, and hands it to his son under the table. Angelo delivers back the tails in short order. Since unlike the others, he is not preoccupied with food, Johnny is first to notice the swaying man approaching their table, holding a beer bottle by its neck. His progress is slow and painful to watch, as his footsteps fall as much to the sides as they do forward. Johnny catches Alejandra's eye and tips his head towards the advancing man in ordinary work clothes.

She springs to her feet but the man is already behind Darby and places one palm on his shoulder for support. The other hand cups Darby's ear and there he deposits a few whispered words.

"Zander, no!" Alejandra commands, fearing the pronouncement he might be making. But it is too late. Darby rises quickly to his feet, knocking over his chair. He twists to take the man by his collar and then launches Zander into the air with surprising force, given his crapulent state. Zander drops his beer bottle in flight and lands hard on his buttocks in a vacant area of the dining room. The bottle, however, shatters upon impact on the tiles, sending shards of glass in many directions, including the area under the table where Angelo is still hiding.

Zak like a freed demon is suddenly in Darby's face. "What the hell are you doing?" she hollers, but is immediately distracted as Johnny pulls a screaming boy from beneath the table, the right side of his perfect face streaked with blood from just above the brow down. Zak presses a clean linen napkin against Angelo's eye and cheek. "I was in the Coast Guard," she tells the boy calmly. "I'm gonna take care of you."

Dee already has their car ready by the front door when Johnny, Allyssa, Zak, and the boy come out. "The hospital's only two minutes away. You follow us," Zak tells Johnny. "Allyssa, you come with us."

Inside the pub, Alejandra attempts to pull Zander to his feet, but keeping him sitting upright with his legs splayed is the best she can do. "What did you say to him?" she asks on her knees now between his legs. She looks directly into his unfocused eyes. "The truth," he blubbers, and buries his face into her chest. "I know, I know," she comforts him, her palms on either side of his head. She had heard only the last of his slurred words and it came out as *shun,* but she knew his intent. "I know," she whispers. "I should have called you."

But this is, after all, Greenport on an ordinary Sunday night in winter, when unexplained things can happen in small spaces. The event, although momentarily interesting to other diners, is not important in any lasting way. This is not a flashy, Hampton's scuffle, although that world is just on the other side of Shelter Island. Here in Greenport, it's not airing dirty laundry when things get ugly in public, it's just dirty laundry left on the floor. Something that you step over. And that is what the overworked waitress does until Dee returns, as the poor woman is forced to cover both zones. After delivering a cool, wet dish towel to Zander, she simply steps over his outstretched legs, applying no pressure to move until he is ready.

Back at the table of ruined dinners, Darby has retaken his seat, facing out into the body of the dining area. His head hangs from his neck with such worrisome weight that Sarah stands and leans her pelvis against his skull, cupping him there like a fetus in distress. She doesn't know what this man Zander whispered into his ear; probably no one heard it but Darby. Quite impressive, though, that Darby rocketed the poor man that high in the air, given Zander's tall, full frame. Between two sober men, she might have given the fight to Zander. But it really wasn't a true fight, she concludes, and there certainly doesn't appear to be a winner.

As Sarah looks over to Alejandra and the man sitting on the floor like a propped-up sock monkey, she wonders what tenuous thread connects them. There seems to be such an imbalance in their relationship, more like mother and child than between two adults. The other diners are back at their bowls of chowder, their beer, and their phones. Finally, a young man with long hair falling over broad shoulders offers to help Alejandra get her comrade up on two feet. The young man wraps his arms around Zander's chest and hoists him upright. They get him back over to his stool at the bar and he seems to perk up a little. He and Alejandra have a short conversation that appears to be a combination of his pleading and her scolding. She turns and walks away while he is still talking.

Halfway back to the table, Alejandra flags down the waitress, folds some money into her hand, and asks that she bring Zander some food and coffee. "Absolutely no more alcohol," she tells her. "He doesn't drink and this is why."

The table is littered with half-eaten meals, but Alejandra sits down and calmly finishes her steak. "I love meat. It signifies success, you know," she tells Sarah. After her plate is clean and wineglass emptied, she adds, "We must go check on Angelo. I see that Zak is back."

Alejandra walks over to Darby, smoothly extracts his wallet from his back pocket, and pulls out a credit card.

"I'll meet you at the car," she says.

CHAPTER ELEVEN • PERMANENT GREEN LIGHT

PERMANENT GREEN LIGHT IS THE COLOR ON THE WALLS OF the waiting room adjacent to the ER. It is the color of the bright optimism of new growth, a blade of grass ushered forth from seed or a tender new leaf. But Darby knows this as well, that it can be a depressing hue when used inappropriately, as it is here, as false as a toothy grin on an undertaker.

He wishes the ceiling were another color, but no, they have chosen to choke them in this tight green cocoon, cramped into miniature chairs. On either side of the uncomfortable seats are cold, aluminum tubes masquerading as armrests. But he's sure they are really there to keep his body from touching the ones next to him, worrisome folk whose anxiety might rub off.

The room is stifling, and he imagines all the bacteria with the lovely Latin names that must be breeding in every warm, moist crevice. Thankfully, someone has opened a window and Darby can smell the salty musk of the Sterling Basin waters. He wonders if he is required to stay.

The artwork is offensive. It's not art at all, but poster reproductions of frightening pastoral scenes painted on the grounds of an insane asylum. He'd like to rip them off the walls, smash them into pieces, and throw them into a dumpster with the other dangerous medical waste.

Darby feels misunderstood. People don't realize the intense unease an artist must endure when thrown into a visually offensive environment. You might as well toss him into a padded service elevator. He begins to sweat and his breathing becomes fast and irregular. He needs a distraction.

On a low table for everyone to enjoy is a collection of outdated magazines, real treasures packed with the inane gossip that people mistake as factual or in any way relevant. Also available are a *Newsweek* dated six months ago, *Highlights* for the kids, and something called *WebMD*, with which he is not familiar, but fears.

Darby looks at his shoes. Worn and familiar, they somehow seem detached from him, there on the 12-inch squares of some false, petroleum-based flooring. He looks above to the naked fluorescent tubes that cast a green pallor onto every face; even Sarah's is the color of deep-forest moss.

Johnny sits across the suffocating, ugly room, as far from Darby as is possible. Still needing distraction, Darby examines the man who gapes at him wide-eyed with nostrils flaring like a racehorse. *He blames me, of course, as if I had taken a knife to the boy's face.* But that thought takes him to Zander and he will not grace the words of that fool with further contemplation.

Darby continues in his appraisal of his supposed adversary, the affable Johnny, stodgy and thick, who is now distracted by Alejandra's comforting whispers. Her arm is draped protectively over his shoulders, all sympathy and seriousness. Darby transfers the image to canvas, painting them as two suffering saints, clutching their robes, eyes to heaven, with halos like fluffed, golden afros. *C'mon, the kid just needs a few stitches. He'll live!*

Even though the irregular gash was practically buried in the boy's eyebrow, they had called in a plastic surgeon to do the suturing.

This required more waiting, so Darby must imagine other paintings to occupy himself. He finds the graceful outstretched form of Sarah on a couch, which is really equal in design and discomfort to three of the chairs, without the middle bars. It has the same faux fabric seats and back. She lies on her side and has made a long pillow with her coat. He's surprised she can sleep here in this public space, something he could never do. How vulnerable she looks there, childlike in her deep slumber. Heartbreaking, what he's put her through, this less-than-married minister. *Did she even have supper?*

This painting would be very different from what he had done earlier in the day. He might just paint the beautiful line that traces shoulder, waist, and hip, what he considers the most feminine contour. Then he might, with subtle blending of transparent tones and ample linseed oil, create a sensuous wash of color. He would blend her form into the the softest of settings, not this antiseptic, lifeless environment, pose her on a red velvet sofa, as would befit such an elegant creature. Naked, primordial. He is aroused by his vision, but is rudely yanked back to reality when a woman in a lab coat opens the door. She's wearing what look like men's eyeglasses and is adorned with a stethoscope around her neck, just so you know to take her seriously. She sits in the empty chair next to Johnny, with Alejandra and soon Sarah in attendance. Darby hears bits and pieces about wound care, follow-ups, how fortunate that...

And then the main event, the little soldier with the gauze pad taped to his face. He marches past Johnny's open arms to the other side of the room to directly face Darby.

Darby takes his tiny hands in case they might be used as weapons against him. "I'm so sorry..."

"You don't have to say that. It was an accident," Angelo consoles him. "Lissa told me you were protecting us. You know, from the strange man."

He said it loud enough for the whole room to hear.

"Allyssa, what?" Johnny blurts, but Darby's hand shoots upward to cut off further comment.

"I would never let anyone harm you," Darby tells the boy, "but I'm no hero. I didn't like what that man said, but I shouldn't have hurt him…or you."

"What did he say?" A simple question from an innocent boy.

"I can't repeat it," Darby explains. "I'll just say he said something about me and my son that I didn't like."

"Then you should have hurt him more. A lot more," Angelo says and pulls his hands free.

Once outside, the caress of a moist harbor air saves Darby. There are papers to be signed and a strong, brave boy to be praised, but the artist is freed from the horrible room and the drama. He watches Sarah alone in his Cadillac, talking into her phone, running one hand over her cropped hair over and over. He will take her back to Orient and hold her tight so she will not run away. They will sleep together until late morning. Only then will he return her to her lost life. And then find, somewhere buried in the pitch and sway of the last few days, his own life again.

CHAPTER TWELVE • IMAGINED YELLOW OF SUNFLOWERS

THE HOUSE ON YOUNGS ROAD YEARNS FOR THEIR RETURN. The storm door had not been properly closed and has been violently banging against the clapboard, chips of white paint falling into the snow. The furnace has been laboring for no one; the refrigerator like a virgin begging to be opened and explored. Beds throw back their covers and field mice in the basement anticipate the happy slogging of feet above and the excess food that will fall to the floor. The wind is growing sharper and more creative as the temperature drops even lower. The house waits, earnestly and loyally, for its reason to exist.

They do not disappoint and arrive in batches. Immediately, Darby cranks the thermostat while Alejandra carries in more wood and restarts the fire in the woodstove.

Johnny had stopped at the only market in town still open and stocked up on snacks and breakfast fare. Now with Allyssa and Angelo, he climbs the stairs to Yago's childhood room where Sarah is already making up the double bed. A colorful hammock is also hanging there, a gift from Alejandra, which is made up to accommodate the boy.

But one unanswered question looms large over the three remaining adults. *Who sleeps with whom?* Darby has over time enjoyed both women in the master bed, but doubts the two would join him there now, something that at one point in his life would have been a huge erotic treat. But the day has felt to him like two. The chill and mass condemnation have hammered his libido. He would most like a long sleep, alone, so offers the bed to the two women. He performs a temporary fix to the headboard and rail, utilizing books and rope. Then finds bedding enough for the couch.

After a raucous popcorn fight in the kitchen, the unconventional family from Brooklyn heads up to bed, with Angelo in Johnny's arms. "What do I call that man?" he asks his father while pointing at Darby.

"Good question. We might need to make up a new name. Or ask him," Johnny says.

Darby is already lying on the couch and has heard the question. He scowls and shrugs in a sort of *whatever* fashion.

"I guess you get to choose then," the father tells his son.

"I have an idea." This from Alejandra who is curled into a rocker in front of the fire. "I love your name for me, *Abuelita,* so there is *Abuelo Abe. Viejo* would also suit him well. But I think good old Grandpa Darby would do just fine."

Darby winces as if slapped in the face, but Angelo sings as Johnny climbs the stairs, "Grandpa Darby, afraid of nobody!"

"I am not that child's grandfather," Darby says to Alejandra, once Angelo is out of earshot. "We have absolutely no blood connection."

"I see," Alejandra answers. "You see families only one way. I disagree. I think love is what defines a family, but I am old-fashioned. I have no appetite for argument, so I will say good night."

As she passes Sarah on the stairs, Alejandra confides, "The *viejo* is all yours."

Sarah joins Darby on the couch. "If you are mine, then wrap me up and keep me warm." Even with the thermostat set above 70 degrees, the wind finds every available port of seepage. Darby sits up and lifts his blankets. She leans her back against him and he brings his arms around her. "This was built as a summer house. Any insulation in these walls is crumpled newspaper."

"I didn't tell you," Sarah says. "I like your painting, but it's a little unnerving."

"A little unnerving?" he whispers in her ear. "That's not what I was going for."

"Maybe that's the wrong word. It's the way you saw me that makes me uncomfortable. What you painted uncovered something that I didn't recognize in myself."

"Need?" Darby asks.

"Very astute, but a certain kind of need."

"Sexual?"

"I had been married a long time. My husband lost interest in sex many years ago. At least with me. I felt nothing for him that way so it was no great loss. We were just friends and that was fine. Or so I thought."

He loosens his hold and begins to massage her neck, his fingers running the length of her spine, across her shoulders, down her arms. "I can't say I've been with a woman long enough to have that problem," Darby says. "I imagine it's a use-it-or-lose-it kind of situation."

"Are you judging me, Abraham? I've had all I need of that," Sarah complains, stopping the movement of his hands. "I think I'd rather call you Abraham, if that's alright with you."

"If you like. And I'm not judging you," he says as he resumes his caressing. "Quite the opposite."

"Abraham, we cannot make love here on this couch with a child upstairs, not to mention Alejandra," she playfully scolds.

"She would enjoy watching."

"Do you want to know my reaction to her painting?"

That slows him down. Again, "If you like."

"It puzzles me. It looks nothing like me."

"Your breasts are much larger," he offers.

"You know, I think the name Darby suits you better."

He feels like they're having two separate conversations. "I admire her work. But, like you, I don't get it. It's always so emotional, fanciful, very female."

"Well, then I should understand it clearly, being female," Sarah says. "I do like her portrait of me, and the watercolor of the young boy there. I don't really have to analyze why."

After awhile she says, "And Abraham Darby, I like you. Probably more than you like yourself right now. Too bad we didn't meet at an easier time."

"We wouldn't have met at an easier time."

"Perhaps. I'm going to bed," Sarah says, rising from the couch and kissing him gently on the mouth.

"Don't let the bedbugs bite," he warns, "or any frisky Costa Ricans for that matter."

‡ ‡ ‡

The bedroom is dark but there is one small candle burning on the bedstand. No shades or curtains cover the two windows and a gentle snow flies erratically in the night sky. Sarah closes the door and leans her back against it.

There will be time to absorb all that has happened. At this moment, she is missing her daughter and the fragments of her life that are still intact. She even misses her husband, not the person so much, but the comforting predictability of him. He had strayed once before, she remembers now, but wasn't that, too, predictable? The brief affair had seemed more traumatic for him. She learned of it soon after it was over, after he had pulled it behind him like a dark, threatening cloud for weeks. It was at the admission of his infidelity that she realized she no longer loved the man. It should have felt more devastating, but she actually had been relieved. It gave a name to the distance between them. Eventually into that void stepped Bennetta. Their collusion, that betrayal, turned Sarah and William's wobbling construct of trust and marriage swiftly into rubble.

So there in the bedroom with the mother of Darby's only child, Sarah rejects any remorse about sleeping with the peculiar man downstairs. She knows that there's little love in it, but a whole lot of something else.

Alejandra is somewhere buried in the heap of blankets and quilts on the bed, leaving no more than a quarter of the space for Sarah. Her eyes are closed but she is not asleep. "Many thoughts," she mumbles. "Any you wish to share?"

"No, what I would like most right now is not to think or share," Sarah tells her in a weary slur. There is a plaid flannel nightgown placed on the bed for her, but Sarah fears it could induce restless dreams of hard life on the prairie. She finds on the floor the soft white shirt of Darby's she had worn earlier and wears only that to bed.

But once horizontal, Sarah can't settle. Her neck is stiff from sleeping on the torturous rack at the hospital. And there's another thing to add to the list of things she thought she'd never do—sleeping like a vagrant in a public space.

Then comes a soothing reassurance in the sound of Johnny's voice in the next room, low and animated, reading to Angelo a book she imagines was once read by Darby to his son. This is the side of Darby she would most like to know, that period when he fathered well and effortlessly. When love for him was unconditional, uncomplicated. She knows he is capable of that. She has felt it more in moments of his absentminded tenderness rather than in his sexual antics.

Then again comes that feeling of being in someone else's life, that feeling she had at his son's funeral, which was only *yesterday*. That dress she had worn belongs to the woman lying next to her, a woman she does not know, but senses, to be naked. It is, after all, the same woman who painted her own breasts and pushed them against a canvas.

Sarah flips from her back to her side, to face Alejandra and the windows with the dancing snow in performance beyond her. The day has been long and exhausting and she should fall asleep easily, but tonight is the third night she lies next to a person she barely knows. Alejandra stirs and apparently has grown too warm under the barrage of blankets as a bare arm thrusts out and falls on Sarah's hip. More of her face is also exposed, and with her makeup washed away she looks much younger to Sarah. Her long, black hair is no longer piled on top of her head, but falls over part of her face and onto her pillow. There lingers still the complex scent of cigar smoke, grilled meat, and a mother's tears.

Sarah watches her twitch in her sleep, thinks of her own daughter, Grace Simone, how she couldn't imagine losing her suddenly, losing her at all. This is what Alejandra bears, yet she sleeps.

"You can touch me if you are curious," Alejandra murmurs, as if in her sleep. "If you do not care to, then we must drift off. I have much to do tomorrow and the thought of being with you is making my sleeping difficult."

Sarah can't move or speak for a long minute, maybe even two. If she does indeed desire her, she wouldn't know where to begin. Alejandra oozes a seductive sensuality to which any living creature would be vulnerable. Finally, although her hand feels like it's raking through thick mud, Sarah manages to push Alejandra's heavy shock of hair from her face, and then allows her fingertips to trace her cheek, touch her parted lips.

"You pity me," Alejandra says.

The puff of air that was the word *pity* nudges Sarah's finger away from Alejandra's mouth, and from the dare and promise embedded there.

"I don't pity you," Sarah says, and instead of admitting her more complicated emotion, adds, "What you're going through frightens me."

"You have children? I forget."

"A daughter. Close to Yago's age."

"It is quite natural to feel pity and fear when death strikes unexpectedly. It's why I was happy to miss the funeral for Yago. I don't want all of that thrown at me. I have much hope."

Sarah falls onto her back. She was once better at this. "Hope?"

"Yes, of course. I believe in an afterlife. I believe I will be reunited with my son. He is waiting for me."

Sarah covers her face with a forearm. "I see."

"Isn't this what you should be telling me, Reverend Obadias, servant of God? This is what your church believes, what you preach to mourners. What you believe, yes? This life is nothing. Bodies are nothing. Yago's, mine, yours, they are all temporary dwellings. Am I not correct?"

Sarah's silence and hiding irritates Alejandra. She sits upright and shakes free Sarah's arm, forcing her to look at her wild hair, narrowed green eyes, and small, noble breasts. Sarah squeezes her eyes shut and shakes her head to free this image.

"You tell me no?" Alejandra persists. "Did you not understand my painting? I told you I was not painting your skin. Not your body!" She is now too agitated to keep still. She throws back all the covers and jumps to her feet. Soon she is standing over Sarah, now a mad, naked temptress.

"Your soul! This is what I painted!" The artist's arms fly in the air above her head. "Breaking free!"

"Free from what?" Sarah asks timidly.

"That is for you to figure out. I cannot paint everything." Alejandra crawls clumsily over Sarah and back under her blankets.

"One more thing before we sleep," she adds. "The great Abraham Darby painted your body, sexy and so sensuous. That is how he knows you and that is fine. He even made *me* want you. It is a beautiful painting. I saw something else."

After a few minutes of complete silence—Johnny no longer is reading and the weary wind rests—Alejandra has a bit more in her. "If you are having trouble with sleeping and orgasm is out of the question, then I can offer you a little taste of marijuana."

"No...no. Thank you. I'll be fine."

"As you prefer."

An hour passes. Sarah is neither fine nor sleeping, but her eyes are closed and her body is more relaxed. She is imagining the two of them lost in a field of fading sunflowers, row upon row, the heavy heads of the flowers resigned to time and gravity. But then, defying nature, their hairy necks stiffen and the flower heads look back to the sun, petals flaring defiantly, seeds pulsing. The sky is a searing blue and the landscape below is awash in pure fiery light. It is breathtaking and she reaches for Alejandra.

"I see it, too," Alejandra whispers into her ear.

"What do you see?"

"This place in your dreams. The vivid colors, so beautiful, yes?"

"Yes." Sarah is past questioning unbelievable things.

"Put a bird there," Alejandra tells her. "Be the bird. Soar above it all."

CHAPTER THIRTEEN • FLAKE WHITE REPLACEMENT
The Fifth Day After Ash Wednesday

SARAH RISES FROM THE BED SHE SHARES WITH ALEJANDRA after hours of broken slumber, both drawn to and terrified of the woman sleeping so soundly beside her. If Sarah could have envisioned herself as a bird in her dreams, that bird would be a tiny, timid sparrow caught in a windstorm.

She dresses in whatever she can find around the room, then wraps herself in a woolen blanket and heads downstairs. By the kitchen door, she slips on boots that are likely Johnny's, heavy black rubber with metal buckles, a type she hasn't seen in years.

Too much wine and inadequate food and sleep have rendered her a little dizzy. The house has grown too warm. She opens the back door and closes it gently behind her. The air feels lusciously alive as she walks down the bluff to the beach. It is neither night nor dawn and the bluish black sky holds both massive clouds and clear patches of equal size. Below that, a churning sea forces more icy chunks to shore. Tiny flakes of snow dance again in all directions, encircling her as she stares east where the appearance of the pale winter sun is promised.

Arriving before that comes a slender form, approaching in bold strides from the east. How odd, she thinks, that another soul would be out here this early in the cold predawn air. The figure comes closer quickly. It is a man broken into hazy lines by the falling snow. He is the near image of a sketch she saw at the funeral party. It was a loose portrait of a young Yago in a black suit with a white shirt, open at the neck. The only color in the image was the brilliant red scarf he wore, which now also graces the figure before her, trailing behind him in the wind.

Now he stands but a few feet away and she turns her head, suddenly aware of her own appearance, an old woman wrapped in a snowy blanket, wearing firemen's boots. She shivers and walks back towards the house.

"Wait," he says. "It's you I've come to talk to."

Sarah turns but comes no closer to him. She sees that his feet are dotted with clumps of ice and snow but are otherwise bare.

"Aren't you cold?" she finally asks, because that simple question is the only one she can formulate right then.

Evidently, the sun is on hold for the time being, but there is heat radiating from him and she no longer feels cold. "You're going to tell me you're Darby's son, aren't you?"

"That may or may not be the case," he tells her.

"Well, you look like the man in his painting," Sarah says, going along with his metaphysical prank. She backs up to an icy boulder. She sits and examines the abstract image in the black suit now a more comfortable distance from her. There is still the heat.

"I sort of feel like a man in a painting. Odd, right?"

Sarah is silent for a moment or two. She looks back at the house. If she had turned on lights, someone else has turned them off.

He continues, unprovoked. "I keep showing up places. I don't choose where. If I'm supposed to be learning something, somebody should tell me what it is."

He grinds his feet into the sand and snow, then kicks into the air and swings his arms around his body. "You know, Sarah, I miss dancing," he says. "Used to make me happy. I miss happy, too."

Just a strange dream, she assures herself, and wills herself to wake. Still, he persists.

"You must have questions for me. I mean, I'm dead!" he shouts. "A dancing dead fag, all dressed up with no palace of heavenly delights to go to."

"I don't actually believe you're here," she says with waning certainty.

"Hey, I can't believe you're actually here. Maybe we're frozen in the same painting. Or in the same dream?" he counters. "But if you have no questions for me, which is really a shame, given your line of work, then I guess I'll just talk. Let me go on about the things from my life that I already miss. Stupid, silly things. Big things, too. I love music and dancing, which I used to be good at, but now I suck. Too self-conscious. And I miss all that shallow stuff that makes life worth living, like sex, rich foods, and laughter. Well, sex, which I can barely remember, ain't so shallow, is it? I mean experiencing another human being in that way, becoming one organism for the sole purpose of pleasure...and occasionally procreation.

"Hey, you're getting cold again. Come here close to me."

Although he is utterly baffling, she is drawn to him in some inexplicable way. She stands, takes two steps towards him, and enters the superheated nimbus which engulfs his physical self.

"Better, right?"

No, she thinks. Or yes? He's not touching her, but she somehow senses his right hand resting on the curve of her left hip, then dropping to cup her pubic bone. She inhales a scorching lungful of air, but does not resist.

"There are most definitely people I hate being away from," he says, "like my son, like Johnny, and my mom. Can't reach them. Like I said, I don't have any say about where I show up."

She's not listening to any of this. She did hear the phrase "the sole purpose of pleasure." Now somehow he has transported her to an unfamiliar state of mindless eroticism. It's surreal, but impossible to detach from. She draws closer to him, intending to caress him in some horrible mix of mothering and lust.

Yago breaks off from her and takes his heat with him.

"Save that for my father," he tells her from a distance. "My poor, fucked-up father. That was a load of dung he dropped on my funeral, right? I know he means well. He's kind of a lovable galoot, isn't he? I think so. We had a little chat while you slept in his Caddy coming out here."

Sarah remembers Darby's odd behavior in the car, that he said he had drifted off but looked so shaken.

"I know things about you," he says teasingly.

"Things about me?" she asks.

"There have to be some perks."

"You know nothing about me," Sarah says.

"Oh ye of little faith."

"You're a punk, even in death. But you, sweet boy, are a mirage. No more real than…"

"You? My father?" he sneers. "That total stranger you spread your legs for? The mad, angry *artiste?* An enigma even to himself."

"Johnny was right about you. You're like a child. You never really grew up."

"Hello, earth to Sarah. Johnny is always right…except in choosing me." His left eyebrow arcs. "Or should it be *heaven* to Sarah. No, I don't think so. Sarah does not believe in heaven. Sarah no longer believes in marriage either. But oh, the minister may marry those willing. She may baptize the innocent and pray over the dead words she no longer believes.

"She's a seller of snake oil. A faithless fraud!" her predatory companion shouts. "You know it! You don't believe in God! Not anymore."

"You can't possibly know this. Leave me alone, Yago. Go back to your netherland. Or maybe hell, if that's where you're headed."

"Yow! Not very Christian," he sings.

"Your faith was a house of cards," he continues. "I love cards, always have a deck on me." He plucks a deck from his left back pocket. He opens the pack and starts flipping cards in the air as he speaks. "Your husband and your beloved mentor each removed a card. Your faithless superiors all grabbed cards. Down came your precious fortress of faith! Left with a meaningless heap of tenets and prayers and ritual, our poor minister leaves her husband of forty-two years, walks away from her closest friend, and is exiled from her congregation. And has it all called a sabbatical! Pretty radical sabbatical, huh?"

"That's enough," Sarah says with her palms over her ears.

"You think I'm only a voice inside your head? Come touch me," he whispers.

Incapable of any response, Sarah looks at the house and sees that Alejandra's bedroom light is on. There's her figure silhouetted in the window, the delicate curve of one hip jutting provocatively to one side.

"I wouldn't venture up there if I were you," he taunts. "What I don't know, dear Sarah, is which died first, devotion to faith or devotion to husband?"

"You don't know anything," she says. "Not what's in my heart, what tortures my soul, what I believe or don't believe. You can't harm me any more than you can help me. This mess in my life is my mess. In time, I will clean it up."

"This illusion of time that you refer to is inspirational for me," he says. "I had the same illusion. Nice to know it survives beyond my short, little life."

That reaches her in a place that is real and frightening. Of course, he is right.

"You know so much?" she dodges in self-defense. "Why is that? Because you're dead, or I suppose more accurately in the process of dying? What this is really all about is not me. Let's talk about you, Yago. Explain, mendacious angel, why the man who brought you into this world, who I imagine cared for and supported you, even when you rejected *him*, how this man can so misunderstand you. Be so ineffectual in his expression of love for you? You must know that, how much he loves you. I barely know him, and I know that. How is it that a man genetically linked could be so emotionally detached? Explain that."

"Easy. He's not my father."

"What?"

"The minister is displaying poor listening skills. Most unfortunate in a minister. But I repeat, Darby's not my father. At least not in terms of DNA. Alejandra told me. I was around 14, maybe even younger. There were many lovers in her life at the time of my unmaculate conception. Mostly men. I mean, look at her. She's still gorgeous, and sexy, don't you think?"

They both look to the window, but Alejandra is gone. Sarah remembers her taunting invitation. *You can touch me if you are curious.*

"But you were too afraid to touch her. Afraid of what you might feel," he teases. "Terrified of the sin you would be committing!"

"He *may* have been your father."

"Nope," he answers quickly. "She knew she was pregnant and hadn't been with him for months. She slept with him immediately and I hung back and arrived a month postmature. Unbelievably, Darby was the most stable man in the bunch. Yes, the drunken, overfed, Nordic master of the arts, Abraham Darby. Key is that he had a rent-stabilized place, some actual income from his paintings and drawings, and a sweetness beneath all the bluster. But you heard him at the funeral! Like he even wanted me in his life. No blood connects us. None!"

"But you look so much like him! It's like they put your mother and Darby in a genetic blender and out came you."

"Out came me. A queer boy with the sensual markings of his mother. My father could be any big-boned bohemian."

"A father is more than a sperm donor," Sarah says formally. "He is the one who fathers." That last line more question than statement of fact.

"Regardless, truth matters," he says. "Listen, Minister, I believe I'm here to help you, not me."

Sarah begins to cry, not from a sense of sadness or despair, but from loss. A deep and universal sense of loss that breaks her and makes her desperate for prayer. But how can she beg God for mercy? When you walk away from God, she is certain that from thence forward, you walk alone.

When Sarah finally sees the muted, disappointing sunrise, the only other inhabitant on the beach is an old, emaciated sea gull, struggling across the sand with a Queen of Hearts in his beak.

CHAPTER FOURTEEN • GAS STATION ORANGE RUST

LIKE A DAZED AND INJURED ANIMAL, SARAH HAS ESCAPED from the beach and all its unearthly torments. When she returns to the quiet house, Darby is deep asleep, the furnace is chugging reliably in the basement, and popcorn still litters the kitchen floor. Abraham Darby is or is not Yago's father and either way, it makes absolutely no difference to her.

Upstairs, the image of Alejandra's exposed bare leg and tousled hair spreading over her pillow is more disturbing. The strands of her hair resemble delicate willow branches laying across a still river in winter. But busy beneath the river's frozen surface, Sarah knows life and desire stir. Dangerous, enticing, simple, yet complicated by the laws of moral behavior. Laws broken every day... *for the sole purpose of pleasure.* Sarah dresses in the near darkness.

Downstairs, she gingerly touches the large and troubled mass that is Darby. Again there is her yearning, but more like the confusing admixture she suffered on the beach. Sarah feels she must leave and it must be now.

Freed from the house on Youngs Road, she takes her first step and then a dozen more. Again and again her boots fall on the icy road. The snowing has ceased and there has been little accumulation.

Where she will go and how she'll get there are of no consequence. It is good enough to be alive, walking alone, wearing one's own clothes, listening to distant bird songs and the reassuring sloshing of traffic ahead.

Whether the apparition was real or only her own malefic, moral demons, it doesn't matter. The cloak of sun has buried the undead in daylight and the biting wind brings clarity to even her clouded conscience. Whatever strange, foreign behavior she has displayed since Friday evening, it has all served to remove the clog in her head, the clog in her life. Every detail—whether in beds, in paints, or in the harsh light of the emergency room, coupled with the lack of proper food and sleep, as well as the abundance of alcohol—all of it now seems flawlessly purposed to this end. Clarity, sometimes induced by prayer or abstinence, can also be found through their opposites. She has proven that.

She carries with her Alejandra's portrait of her, freed of its wooden frame, and rolled into a large plastic garbage bag. *Be the bird.* Well, the bird has flown and she takes the final steps to the Main Road.

There Youngs Road ends and she must choose left or right, east or west. To the right is the long and windy causeway, East Marion, then Greenport, the Lookout, the harbor, the hospital. Left is something else, something unchartered. So left it is. That is where the gauzy pink sun is. And perhaps a coffee shop. A bus.

She stops abruptly as she hears the words of the deconstructed image on the beach. *Truth matters.* She flips up the collar of her coat, stamps snow from her boots. She's lived in a world of lies for too long…lies in her marriage, lies in her ministry, not being honest even to herself. Of course, truth matters. But its nature is as amorphous as that apparition early this morning.

Not even a half mile down the road, Sarah comes upon a round sign looming larger than the sun it blocks. With bold lettering in rusty orange paint, it reads only GAS, nothing more. Back from the road, there is a small one-room office with two bays on the right for repair work. Directly in front of the office, a man is bent over the engine of a small pickup. He seems to sense her presence and stands and turns to face her. It takes her a moment to place him and when she does, she looks away and hastens her pace.

"Wait," he shouts. "Hold on there. I know you."

Sarah stops but doesn't turn around. *Will she never be free of the spreading influenza that is Darby's life?*

He runs up to her, wiping his hands on an oily rag and then thrusting his right one at her, "Alexander Whelan. I don't remember a lot of last night, but I remember you."

Sarah removes her glove and takes his slick, thick hand in hers.

"I remember you, too, but not that name."

"Those people call me Zander. I prefer my given name, but that's the one that's stuck in their heads from a long time ago."

"How are you?" she asks. She doesn't care at all how he is or how he's dealing with what must be a pretty impressive hangover.

"I gave up drinking years back."

"I see," she says. That was not what she asked, but it doesn't matter.

"I mean, maybe that's why I didn't handle it so well. I guess I sort of blacked out. I do remember being airborne and in Alejandra's arms. And that Yago's boy got cut up. Is he okay?"

"Needed some stitches. He'll be fine."

"Zak drove me home in my truck. I have no idea how she got back," Alexander says, hanging his head. "I'm pretty devastated about Yago. I knew he had AIDS, but I figured he was living with it okay. Can I ask you something?"

An uncomfortable silence follows. She looks at the tiny office. "You have any coffee in there?"

"Just put some on," and he motions for her to follow.

The office surprises Sarah. It's warm, very warm, and actually cozy. There's the obligatory clipboard of handwritten service orders and shelves of manuals, catalogs, and phone books. There's a cash register from another time and a credit card apparatus, outdated as well. But also, on the floor, there's a worn Persian rug, and a beautiful, old pine desk sits beneath the front window. The top is scattered with a dictionary, thesaurus, many notebooks, a stack of papers, and a soup can filled with pens and pencils. In the corner, an overstuffed chair holds a plaid blanket and bed pillow, where he likely spent the night.

"Now tell me something about you," he says astutely as he pours her coffee. Cream appears from a small refrigerator and some honey in the shape of a plastic bear.

"You're a writer?" Sarah asks, removing her coat and gloves.

"Guilty. Short stories. You're surprised? Thought I was just some hick mechanic?"

"I thought mechanic but no further." The coffee is strong and good. She is grateful and so adds, "You have a question for me?"

Alexander offers her the chair, removing his bedding first. He takes the chair at his desk, pours his own coffee. He adds a lot of cream and a couple of squirts from the honey bear.

"What the hell are you doing with Abraham Darby?" He smiles.

"Before I answer that, may I ask how you know him, well, all of them I'm guessing?"

"I lived in the city in my early twenties. Was part of Alejandra's circle, which included Darby. Thought I could paint. I had absolutely no talent for it or so everybody kept telling me. But I loved the lifestyle. Sex, alcohol, drugs, parties that lasted for days. We brought that all out here, too. But once Alejandra had deserted us for the rest of the world, I just stayed here. Orient better suits a writer's solitary life. Your turn."

"Let's just say I'm a runaway. Starting over. Almost seventy and starting over. Funny, right? I was running away and I ran into Darby," Sarah says, hoping he won't ask what she was running from.

"We all go through changes. Where are you headed now? I mean, where's home? I didn't see a car."

"I don't own a car. I live in Manhattan."

A car pulls up to the pump out front. "I'll be right back," Alexander says, and tapping the stack of papers on the desk adds, "How about you read the one on top."

He calls out "Walter!" as he opens the door. She watches as his curly head of graying sandy hair pokes into the car's interior. He tugs on the brim of the driver's cap and they begin a lively conversation.

She has no desire to chat or even read his probably sad little story. Still, she realizes that he could be her ticket on her first leg home. Sarah walks over to the desk and takes the top few sheets of handwritten manuscript. The tidy lines of ink on looseleaf paper evidence a fastidious and careful author. Since gas has not yet entered Walter's tank, she pours more coffee and returns to her chair to read the following tale:

WILL THE BOY DROWN?

Alexander Whelan 1978

A man was planted in a aluminum chair on the beach. In his hands, a small sketch pad and a dull drawing pencil. At his side was a tall glass.

A young boy, with a mass of wet, dark curls dangling, stood a mere four feet from the shoreline. He wore white little boy briefs, as the bathing trunks could not be found.

It was an ordinary mid-August day, hot and hazy, a little past four.

The boy kicked his right foot in the water repeatedly.

Drops of airborne salt water danced in the diffused light. The boy embraced the water with open arms, palms pulling the foamy liquid to his face.

With his head snapped back, the man drained his glass. He stared at the white sky and slipped lower in his chair. He felt a rare contentment. As he savored the heat of the sun, he exhaled a noisy yawn and then returned his focus to the water.

Sarah walks to the door, still holding the manuscript. It was only Saturday night that Darby talked about this incident, or one much like it. In reality, the boy does not drown, but what ending will this mechanic favor. He's actually pumping gas now, but still engaged with Walter. She continues reading.

But where was the boy? Not in the shallow surf or on the beach in either direction. Was not visible in the suddenly violent deeper water. The man battled his way out of the low armless chair. He charged the water and was soon waist-deep. Walking in the water was useless so he dove aimlessly about until, miraculously, he saw the boy tumbling to shore. He ran awkwardly to him and gathered his son into his arms.

The boy coughed and breathed in shallow gulps. "I knew I'd find you," the man lied as he folded him into his blanket of flesh.

Over the years, the man would repeatedly ask himself if that was what truly happened. He knew he often couldn't remember in much detail what happened even the day before. He gradually over time learned to forgive himself for his careless disregard for this most precious child.

Still, it took many years.

But on that summer afternoon, those baffling thoughts were for the future. He lowered the boy to the sand, scolded him for his disrespect for the power of the sea, and confined him to the beach to play. He was just as fine to sketch that way.

Alexander opens the door and lays a twenty dollar bill on his desk.

"You don't care much for Darby, do you?" Sarah says, laying the papers on the desk. "He's the father here, and the boy…the boy is Yago."

"That was one of my first stories. Never published, which is a blessing because it's so poorly written. I read it again last night."

Sarah is putting on her coat. "Thanks for the coffee."

"Please don't go. Not yet," he says. "I'm probably the only person you've met these last few days who wants nothing from you."

"But you want me to stay."

"You know, I don't even know your name."

"Reverend Sarah Obadias," she says formally and lays her coat on the back of the chair and sits. She feels more tired than anything else and the excessive heat in the room is making her sleepy.

Alexander takes from a desk drawer a round loaf of bread dusted with white flour. With a serrated knife from the same drawer he cuts on a wooden board four thick slices from the center. Then from a shelf next to four volumes with his name on the spines, he selects a Mason jar and from it slathers some gritty peanut butter onto two slices. A generous amount of raspberry jam from another jar completes the sandwiches. He offers one to Sarah on a paper napkin saying, "Gifts of God for the people of God."

She devours the thing in exactly the same fashion as she would have 65 years earlier, eating first the soft center, then licking the oozing contents from the edges of the bread. When she comes up for air, she sees that Alexander has taken only a couple of bites.

"Tell me, how did he die," he asks.

"He had a heart attack."

"Was he alone?"

"I don't know." Sarah would like to recommend that Alexander go down to the beach just before daybreak. There he can ask the undead all the questions he likes. "You were close?"

"Not really. I was very close to his mother."

"Alejandra?" She remembers them on the floor of the Lookout. Her strained patience, his little boy adoration.

Another car at the pump removes Alexander from the room for a short time. He's abrupt when he returns. "Did you sleep with her, too?"

"With Alejandra?" This break in polite conversation jars her. "No! I mean, yes, we slept in the same bed. That's all."

"I'm really sorry. That was an inappropriate question, especially to a minister."

"I was a minister."

"Retired?"

"No," Sarah says with irritation, wondering when she will no longer have to endure the same questions. "I'll tell you flat out. Inappropriate things happened. I did inappropriate things in response. I became a stranger to myself. I lost my faith and did not hide it well."

"Tell me more," he asks.

Of all the places to let this out, she has chosen the cramped office of a gas station with a literary mechanic she does not know at all. But there is no reason not to; and in telling him, perhaps it will make more sense to her. So Sarah indulges—this room has now become her confessional and he will be the earnest and forgiving priest.

"One Sunday morning not long ago, I told the God-loving people in the pews before me that I had lost trust in the institutions that had always fortified me. I questioned the nature and even the existence of a loving God. Believe me, this is not what I wanted at this point in my life. I longed for the faith I once had, the unquestioning faith of my parents. I was born into it, breathed it; it was a very real part of who I was."

His chin rests on his fingertips. "What happened?"

"Imagine if you stopped believing in what you loved...or who you loved. Alexander, no more writing, no more Alejandra. You'd feel empty and lost, wouldn't you?"

"If I couldn't write," he says, "I would have to find a new way to think. It's how I understand my life."

"There were things my husband and I should have discussed but they went unsaid. We just stuck to the small stuff and often bickered. I didn't realize how unhappy he was. Then, sure enough, not long ago, my closest ally in life, the woman I confided in without restraint, without thinking, whether the subject was church or marriage related, this woman, Bennetta, esteemed professor in the Department of Religion at Columbia..."

"You don't have to tell me this," Alexander squeezes into her pause. "I mean, I sense what's coming."

"They sat me down in my own living room, Bennetta and William, my William, and told me about their relationship, the accident that had happened virtually against their will. What total bullshit. I immediately threw up on the only decent rug I own. And walked away from them both."

Alexander crosses his arms and drops his head.

"I'm sorry. This is all so bleak," Sarah says, feeling her confession has inflicted a wound, although she knows betrayals such as this are commonplace.

"I've told no one," she admits. "Not my daughter or the head pastor of my church. I felt so angry but also ashamed. I did. To lose them both. *What had I done?* I had to walk away.

"Two weeks later I was in a very small apartment by myself, with only a world of doubt to keep me company. My husband agreed to a legal separation. He sends brief letters. I write back but don't send them. My daughter blames me for the breakup and rarely calls me now.

"My behavior became even more erratic. Listen to this. Last week I saw some young, arrogant punk on the street harassing this girl, using the usual epithets boys that age favor to diminish girls who reject them. He wouldn't stop and the girl was crying and backing into the building behind her. I went up in his face like a crazy woman, a full head taller than he was. I grabbed him by his collar and slapped him hard across his astonished face. I screamed at him to make more of himself than just an ass."

Alexander goes over to the small refrigerator and pulls out a couple of beers. It's not yet 8:30.

"I thought you didn't drink anymore," the minister comments.

"I'm turning over a new leaf. Go on."

She takes her bottle, then his, and returns them to the refrigerator.

"His friends all started laughing at him, jeering that some old black woman had just taken him down," she continues. "The kid threw back my arms. I could see he was considering the ramifications of hitting me back, but he was the more mature of the two of us. He stepped away from me, palms out, like I was a dangerous virus. What he did shout at me I would rather not repeat, but it was no worse than what I shot back at him. I was no hero to the girl either. She went over to the kid to check on his injured face. She *consoled* him! People stopped and watched. I was completely out of control."

She wishes that she had that beer. There's a little cold coffee in her mug so she drinks that. "Am I scaring you?"

Someone is honking out front. "Let me get him set up," Alexander says. "Told him he could use the lift to do a brake job."

She paces the room in his absence. *Will this purging help?* She wonders what else will fly out of her mouth. *Should she politely return the conversation back to his life?*

But Alexander has barely sat down again when Sarah selfishly resumes.

"Last Sunday was my day to preach and I dug out an old sermon entitled "God and Reason." It was scholarly and well-intentioned, if not inspirational. I stood before my congregation—and some of those people I had known for decades—and from my mouth came not a word from the sermon in front of me. Except for the title. For the next fifteen minutes or so, everything I put out there was in the form of a question, at first quite benign and then increasingly accusatory."

"What were the questions?" Alexander asks.

"What is sin? Is God a salve for our wrongdoing? Is faith a way to defend against the finality of death? Can the Bible be believed with all its bigotry and condemnation? What assurance do we have of God's love? What assurance do we have of even his existence?

"At first they just smiled, nodding their heads from time to time. Then came the fidgeting. They kept expecting me at some point to provide answers to these questions, thought that this was some rhetorical introduction to the assuaging message I usually pumped out."

"Dear minister, don't be so hard on yourself," he comforts. "Your questions are the questions many people in those pews have asked themselves. Didn't even Jesus cry out to his father, 'Why hast thou forsaken me?'"

"When I finished my sermon, I simply left the church," Sarah says, ignoring him. "I met with the church hierarchy last Wednesday.

They were patient, although very condescending. Offered me a sabbatical, some time to sort things out."

Sarah retrieves the plastic bag she had tucked next to her chair. She pulls out the canvas, unrolls it, and shoves it in his face, like an angry protester with a handmade sign.

"It's Alejandra's," he says. "I would know her work anywhere."

"It's of *me!* Do you know why my face is a ghostly white?"

Now she is starting to look a little crazy to him. He examines all the elements of the painting, the fluid brushstrokes like the wake of a small boat, all the pungent oranges with their citrus scent, the reds like fresh blood, the whole visceral quality so common in her work. He would often miss the actual representation, the what or the who in the painting, so lost he'd become in her method, her vivid palette, and her mind.

"Does it matter?" he asks after some time.

She sits in the large chair and tries to calm herself. "The dead are calling me."

"Your face is painted white because the dead are calling you? Couldn't you also say that she painted a light within you greater than the darkness around you?"

"That is a poetic and writerly interpretation," she tells him. "Last night in bed we talked about what the painting meant. She claims she was painting my soul, my soul freed. I can't even begin to tell you what happened to me on the beach this morning before dawn. I'll just say that I hungered after a younger man, chasing him down in his afterlife. But all that doesn't matter. What matters is this...the dead are calling me."

He thinks this would be a nice time to have a car pull up to the pump. *Gas, please. Here's your gas. Here's your money. Done.* But there is no car. So they must continue discussing the one topic guaranteed to make anybody squirm.

"Both my parents died before ever receiving a Social Security check. I had one brother. He was a First Lieutenant, 44th Artillery, Army. He was killed in Vietnam. He was 20.

"I think the dead are calling me...as they called Yago."

"I can't believe he's gone," Alexander tells her, his eyes unfocused.

"I can't command myself to believe in God, in his mercy, his church," Sarah says, seeming not to mind his lack of attention. "I wish I could because I want to believe. I want there to be something more. The deeper I look the less I find. There is nothing to sustain me. When I lost my faith, I lost a huge piece of who I am."

"Sarah, you are obviously an intelligent woman. Please listen to me. You don't look like you're on death's doorstep. If you've lost something so intrinsically tied to your well-being, you need a plan to find it again."

"A plan? Really?" She walks over to the side window, runs her index finger down the oily glass. "Like a plan to lose weight? A savings plan? Retirement plan? I've had a life of plans." She faces him. "What's your plan? What have you lost and how do you plan to get it back?"

"I want Alejandra in my life again, and my plan is to wait until she tires of jumping from one lover to the next."

"Ha! What are you, seventeen? I mean no offense, but that's not a plan. That's a dream."

"And what's the difference between the two?" he wants to know.

"A plan is a concrete course of action," she explains. "A dream is... just fantasy."

"Really? I know that I have loved no other woman since the day I met her. Yago kept me tied to her. Another reason I live here is because I know I'll see her from time to time." He looks down, shakes his head. "I don't know if that's still true."

"A dream, sweet, very romantic. But still a dream," Sarah says coldly.

"Didn't you dream of becoming a minister before you did the work to become one? Did you ever dream of becoming a mother when you were a young girl? Dream of falling in love?"

Sarah suddenly yearns for her small apartment, her own bed, to telephone her daughter. "Please, Alexander Whelan, could you get me to a train or a bus back to Manhattan?"

He waits, looking intently at her. Then, smiling, "Yup. I'll just lock up. But listen, I'm just an average writer—and a gifted mechanic, I might add—but I know you've got to separate your mind from your heart to fall in love. I mean, it's not a rational thing to do. And I know that faith is similar, based on love and trust, not thought.

"I mean, be honest with me. You walked in here needing a ride," he adds while he pulls schedules from a desk drawer, "and look how long it took you to ask for it."

Twenty minutes later, Alexander leaves her at the Jitney bus stop in Greenport. Before he leaves her, he is compelled to add further instructions. "Put away your fear, Sarah. Wear your faith, no matter how worn and full of holes it is. Love every thing and every human being you can and you'll love your way back to God."

Ridiculous, she thinks. *As if it were that simple.*

He pauses, knowing that she has dismissed his advice. "But what do I know? I'm just a love-struck mechanic, right?"

CHAPTER FIFTEEN • BURNT UMBER

THE REMAINING INHABITANTS OF THE HOUSE ON YOUNGS Road have fallen victim to the predatory nature of sleep upon those whose lives have been pummeled by fate. Each in his or her dreamlessness has longed to be nourished by an unfettered detachment from reality, here being the loss of someone much loved. Bodies have remained motionless well past daybreak.

Nature has also encouraged the long hours of slumber by administering both a threatening, slapping wind and a display of massive purple clouds overhead to blur the transition from night into day.

A full belly of oil feeds the furnace below and there had seemed no present or urgent reason for them to initiate the day. Only Angelo had risen for a brief time to gather a few of Yago's childhood treasures that were still lining the open shelves between the windows. Things that Yago had touched and played with many times seemed, even to a boy Angelo's age, to be made more valuable by his passing. They were now also ownerless and so Angelo had sat on the floor making small piles of plastic trucks and soldiers, playing cards, and board games. There were books, books that Yago had read to him, that the boy opened and smelled and touched reverentially. Death remains for him a huge unknowable thing, as does the concept of heaven, which seems to him like a slightly scary place and he fears Yago is alone and missing his son.

Angelo had eventually selected the softest and most comforting artifact he could find, a worn, stuffed penguin, and then crawled into Allyssa's arms.

Back in the master bedroom, Alejandra again had feigned sleep and watched through the slits of peeping eyes as Sarah hunted for clothes a second time and dressed before her. Gentle pangs of arousal had warmed Alejandra's groin and she realized how common it was for her to have lubricious attractions to Darby's women. Some raw, animalistic appetite for new lovers haunted them both. Although Sarah was different than the others, she shared with them that powerful double punch of a well-endowed physique and refined intellect. But knowing that any liaison between them must fall to another less complicated time, Alejandra had let her go without even a goodbye.

Darby had been stirred by Sarah's meek touch and then secretly watched her exit the room, as if she were leaving the scene of a crime. He saw her lean against the kitchen door, pulling on her leather boots, then wrapping her white coat around her. The gifted scarf she had left behind. When she lingered by the open door, the wind rushing into the room, he had hoped she would return to him, or at least leave a note or a number. But when she walked back into the front room, it had not been for him, but for Alejandra's painting, which she took back into the kitchen. On went the lamp on the countertop, drawers opened and closed, many faint, prying sounds, then the snap of plastic. And she was gone.

He could have broken free of the torturous couch, never intended for a man his size. Could have thrown on his trousers, shirt and shoes, ran after her. Pulled her back into his chaotic life. *But why?* He quickly realized that if she had wanted to stay here with him, she would have.

He had looked across the room and seen his painting, which she had left behind. Sad the way the woman there beckoned to him. Even sadder was that the painting was all he had of her.

His last thought before he willed himself back to sleep was a wish that the house be empty when he woke.

‡ ‡ ‡

Well past ten, Johnny descends with his son in his arms, legs dangling, his left cheek against his father's shoulder. The white square of gauze on the other side of his face a reminder to all, except Angelo, of Darby's foolish carelessness.

"We're going out to breakfast. Then we have to get back to Brooklyn," Johnny tells Darby, who is still half-asleep.

Angelo is excited about this plan. "We're going to the Pancake House! Do you want to come with us?"

"No, Darby's busy today," Johnny tells Angelo. "He can't go."

Allyssa comes stumbling down the staircase, laden with bags, a pillow, the stuffed penguin. A barechested Darby sits up, combs his hair with his fingers. "You bought all that food."

"Enjoy," Johnny says.

Angelo scrambles away from Johnny and walks over to the couch. "Can I have these? They were Papa's." In his hands are three decks of playing cards in yellowing, perfect boxes.

"Sure. Sure you can," Darby says. "Take whatever you want."

"Really?" His eyes are bright as headlights. "I want the trucks and..."

"No!" Johnny takes the boy's hand and leads him towards the kitchen. "That's all we're taking."

"Just one truck? Please?" Angelo pleads.

"Another time," Darby says, wondering when that other time might possibly be. So he dresses quickly and goes up to his son's old bedroom. He does not like being in there; it's too soon. *Why hadn't they cleaned out this stuff long ago?* He takes a pillow from the unmade bed and shakes it out of the pillowcase. From the shelves he grabs books, toys, a pair of binoculars, and fills the pillowcase.

When he gets back downstairs, the little family is already in coats and hats, with Johnny wearing his ridiculous galoshes. Darby sits in a chair near the door. "Come here, Angelo."

The boy breaks free of his father's hand and stands stiffly in front of Darby.

"I want you to have these things," Darby tells him. Then looking at Johnny, "This is between you and me. Yago would want you to have them. What would I do with them?"

He opens the pillowcase so Angelo can see. "I'll share them with you, if you want," the boy says earnestly, taking the bag from Darby.

"Just say thank you, Angelo. Let's go," Johnny says, opening the door.

"Can't get away from me fast enough?" Darby quips to Johnny.

"Tell Sarah bye from us," Johnny says.

"There is no Sarah here to receive your message," Darby says. "She has flown."

"Wise woman. Bye, Abe." And then Johnny and crew are gone.

But because this flippant hostility is foreign to Johnny, it unsettles him. He sits in the driver's seat, staring out into the grey water of the Sound.

"What's wrong?" Allyssa asks.

Johnny shakes his head. "That's not right," he says and he jumps out of the car, leaving his door open.

Back in the kitchen, Darby is making coffee and is startled by Johnny's abrupt entrance.

"Listen," Johnny says, framed in the door like a saint on a holy card, "I know it was an accident. You're going through a lot. I'm sorry if I'm making this any harder on you."

No reply is needed and he ducks back out again.

On cue, Alejandra arrives in the kitchen minutes later, dressed and harried. She, too, goes straight for her coat.

"No coffee?" Darby has already placed two mugs on the counter.

"I cannot believe how late it is. Thank God Johnny knocked on my door. How could you let me sleep so long?"

"Where is the goddamn fire?" Darby pours her coffee. "Sit and have breakfast with me."

"Where do you suppose our minister friend has wandered off to, with no car or even a map to direct her?" she says, ignoring his directive and wrapping her scarf around her head. "She is troubled, but interesting, yes? Will we see her again?"

"No. I have no way to find her, no phone number, and I know nobody that knows her. I don't even know how to spell her last name. And that's fine. I have no time for women. I have work to do."

"Of course. You always have work," she says. "We, Johnny and I, are going to sort through some of Yago's things later in the week. Maybe you want to join us? I will call you."

"Don't. There's nothing I want."

"At some point, you may change your mind. But for now, goodbye my darling Darby. I'm here two weeks. Call me, for dinner, anything. Maybe just to talk? Will you do that for me?"

Darby looks lost. On tiptoes she kisses his unshaven cheek. "Paint," she tells him before closing the door behind her. "Just paint. That is how you understand everything."

Then it is Darby who hurries to leave, hating the accusatory, hollow hum of the empty house. He empties the fridge into a paper sack that he intends to throw away. The trash in a plastic bag beneath the sink is placed in his trunk to be deposited in the Riverhead McDonald's waste bin, per his custom. He turns the thermostat back to 50 degrees.

Darby rips the sheets and blankets off the beds, and as he flings the sheets from the master bedroom into his laundry basket, out flies a pair of Sarah's skimpy underpants. Darby had not noticed them when she had stood before him in his loft days ago. They are not of the sort, he assumes, that most female ministers wear. The material is silky in his hands and they are a brothel red. Or—and this thought is even more bothersome—do they simply belong to Alejandra?

Darby sits on the bare mattress with the mysterious garment and remembers what Sarah had said just last night, that she'd been married a long time, that one of them had lost interest. But why would she wear something like this if she was not interested in sex? *Was she being honest with him?* Were there others as inconsequential as he most likely is?

He wasn't seriously entertaining the idea of having sex on the couch with her last night, but she was! *What happened when she went upstairs?* He tries to remember Alejandra's demeanor this morning. She was certainly evasive. And she had asked if *they* would see Sarah again, this troubled but interesting woman.

Darby shoves the underpants into his trouser pocket. He feels betrayed by this woman he claims not to care about. He leaves the sheets in the basket. Random clothes are thrown into another plastic bag.

Then there is the matter of his painting, the one which remains on the floor of the front room, left behind like an unpleasant odor. He tucks it under his arm and then locks the door upon leaving.

As he places the portrait of the sensuous minister next to him in the Cadillac, he sees wedged in the seat a cell phone, simple, black, and ministerial. *Sarah's.* He powers it up, quickly scrolls through the contacts, then turns it off and drops it in his pocket next to her undergarment.

If she has run away, she has left a trail.

CHAPTER SIXTEEN • ECCLESIASTICAL GOLD HAZE

FATHER WILLIAM GUYTON IS UNFAMILIAR WITH ANY BROOKLYN neighborhood beyond Brooklyn Heights and needs to refer to a subway map to locate Court and Carroll streets. Once there, he is dismayed to find five restaurants within a block each way of that intersection.

There is a small park, fenced in, but the gates are open. Teenagers huddle around a music player, smoking. Old men, though not that much older than Father Guyton, play bocci ball and sip from paper cups. It's early evening, that blessed time of day when he generally shifts from what is work to what is not, from the public to the private, but this is not the case on this day. The good priest settles on a cold bench to ponder his next move.

The previous two nights had been most strange for him. In order to deliver what he must to Yago Díaz, he had to locate his residence, as in all their time together, no address or phone contact was offered. Now their work was done and he doubted Yago would be looking for him. So he had set out from the protective fortress of his massive white church on Sixth Avenue to either find him or someone who knows him.

The first location he chose had been a disaster. Not that the men were unfriendly, but he had felt like a loose monkey or an exotic tiger, any sort of creature that would not fit into a gay West Village bar. In his white collar, highly polished oxfords, and a part in his hair reminiscent of an Arizona desert highway, he did not present well. He had ordered a Merlot (another mistake) which he found to be undrinkable. One young man broke up his buddies with "Did the pope send you?" and another cruelly asked him if he was searching for good-looking altar boys. But most were polite and guarded, offering no information about someone they claimed not to know.

He had returned to the rectory on Waverly Place and had poured himself a healthy glass of a superior wine.

The next night was Sunday and he had headed out earlier to another bar which was also a restaurant. The clientele confirmed its gay bent and he found a barstool that was unoccupied. He was soon happily served a very decent Cabernet. There was a grand piano tucked into the corner and the ambiance was warm and lively. He had a long conversation with a middle-aged fellow in a bow tie concerning the writings of St. Augustine, which later led to the New Testament and current laws in the state of Florida regarding gay adoption. He had found the man pleasantly engaging and later discovered that he, too, was Catholic.

When Father Guyton finally got around to the subject of Yago—of whom the man claimed no knowledge—they could barely hear each other as the entire room had joined a solo singer in "What's New Pussycat?" When Father Guyton found himself belting out the infamous *Whoah-Whoah-Whoe* he knew he must leave.

He then walked further west down that same street to a darker, less-populated area. There were a few establishments there, nameless and with curtained or shuttered windows. He was not frightened, but just to be on the safe side, he made a quick sign of the cross and knotted his scarf over his collar.

The dark interior was dotted with a few men and he plopped down onto yet another barstool. He waited for the bartender to slowly disengage from a group of serious-looking fellows, wearing what appeared to be western-style clothing. When he was finally asked what he'd like to drink, Father Guyton got right to the point. *Did he or any of his customers know Yago Díaz and if so, possibly supply a phone number or an address?*

The bartender had shrugged, but took the long walk to the other end of the bar and spoke to the men there. Two just shook their heads but a third leaned closer. He whispered into the bartender's ear and then took a pen from a pouch on his waist and jotted something down on a cocktail napkin.

After another slow saunter back to Father Guyton, the bartender crossed his arms and asked how he knew Yago. The priest simply untied his scarf, revealing his white collar. He told him that he was a close friend.

"Well, if you're such a close friend, you'd know that he ain't around anymore. He lived above a restaurant in Brooklyn. That guy doesn't remember the name of it but it's near this corner." Then the barkeep shoved the napkin at him.

"But where did he go?" The priest was taken aback. He had just seen Yago a few days earlier.

"Far, far away. Now you want a drink or not?"

Father Guyton slid off his stool, took two singles from his wallet, and laid them gently on the bar. The bartender muttered something and shoved the meager tip into his pocket.

Now the priest must complete his crusade and safely deliver to Yago's home what is tucked in the inside pocket of his winter coat.

The first restaurant near the designated corner is quite fancy, upscale Italian. The woman at the door knows of no one by that name. The next attempt looks more bohemian and so more promising. A pungent aroma inside is a cinnamony apple sweetness. The young waiter he speaks to does know Yago. He tells the priest that he is so sorry about what happened. "I see lights on across the street so I think he's open. Please give Johnny our love," he tells him with a sugary sadness.

Standing in front of the small, appealing bistro with the lovely stained glass windows, the priest for the first time imagines just how far away Yago may be. He ventures inside.

The restaurant is devoid of diners but filled with a lovely operatic voice. The amber light pulls him further in and he edges closer to the kitchen door in the far back. Then he hears a chorus of voices, male and female, with an orchestra whispering behind them. The scent of thyme and onion and mild fish, combined with the seductive lighting, the rich music—it all creates a mournful loveliness, so intimate, as intimate as grief, he fears. He feels he is invading this intimacy and turns to go. But then he hears the winsome giggling of a boy and through the open kitchen door rolls an onion, its papery skin falling off as it travels directly to the priest's shoes. The child chasing the runaway vegetable stops abruptly.

"Food is not a toy until it is in your mouth," someone teasingly shouts from the kitchen.

"We're not open yet," the boy announces. "Daddy's still cooking."

"And you must be…" the priest asks with much tenderness.

"Have a seat, Father," Johnny says from the doorway. "You're in luck. It's Monday and that means risotto! And it's seafood risotto tonight. My specialty!" Taking his arm he leads his guest to the family table.

"My name is Father William Guyton. I'm looking for Yago?" A question to which he fears he knows the answer.

"Yago died last week."

The priest knows well the words that would be appropriate but says nothing. Whatever contentment was in the room, he has wiped it clean away. He pulls back a chair and sits.

"I'm Johnny. His widower. We were married. This is Angelo, our son. Not a family in the eyes of the Catholic Church. You are a Catholic priest, yes?" he asks.

"Guilty. Yes."

"Angelo, please return the onion to the kitchen and continue with the letter *f*." The boy backs into the other room.

"And close the door. Please."

Once they are alone, Johnny sits directly across from the priest. "I heard about you, Father."

"Please give me a moment to explain."

"*You* were the priest he was seeing."

"We met many times."

Johnny is confused and not sure how to navigate through the cloud of questions in his head. "You knew he was gay?"

"I'm no expert but I would think even his holiness the Pope would have recognized that about him."

"You're not being clear about your relationship with Yago. Were you sleeping with him or trying to de-gay him?"

"Good God! No! Neither. Why are you thinking I'm your enemy, John?"

"John?"

"That's your given name, isn't it? Yago referred to his partner as John."

"We were married. I was his husband. He was mine. And everyone calls me Johnny, except for my son. Yago called me Johnny. What *was* your relationship with him?"

The priest folds his hands and rests his elbows on the linen table-cloth. He leans forward, closer to Johnny. "We rarely talked about his being homosexual. I think I can tell you that he told me he was celibate, had been for quite a long time."

"So it wasn't just me he was avoiding," Johnny says and then adds without provocation, "But he was so affectionate. It was his nature."

"Yes. He had a very warm heart, I could tell that. But very hard on himself. Very vulnerable and easily hurt," Father Guyton says.

"You are avoiding my question. What did you want from him?" Johnny sits back in his chair.

"What did I want from him? He came to *me*. Yago was in great distress. He came to me for comfort…for his soul. Maybe he knew."

"That makes no sense. Why would he seek comfort from a Catholic priest? My son and I go to an Episcopal church almost every Sunday. We know a priest there really well. Even Yago knew him a little. Why wouldn't he go to him?"

"I can't answer that. He never mentioned your faith…other than telling me that you were raised Catholic."

Johnny stands and tiptoes over to the closed kitchen door. He gently swings it back but it immediately meets the toes of Angelo's sneakers.

"As I suspected," his father says.

"I'm done with *f*," Angelo announces.

"Then do your numbers."

"I did that."

"Angelo, occupy yourself. Has Allyssa come down yet?"

"Yep."

"Ask her to check the risotto and start a salad. *Now get!*"

He turns his attention back to his visitor. "I was raised Catholic but the Catholic Church has no use for me. It does not accept who I am. It invalidates our relationships."

The priest has sympathy for his plight. "The church has rules, laws that are not arbitrary, but are based on the laws of the Bible. But the words and teachings of Christ were always grounded in love and forgiveness."

"I know that. Maybe you should try to convince the church hierarchy to show a little love and forgiveness. Anyway, forgiveness implies wrongdoing, doesn't it?"

"John, I'm not here to judge you. I undertook some rather laughable excursions into your community to find Yago's home, to find you, and to give you this." Father Guyton reaches into his heavy coat and presents to Johnny Avitabile the certificate of baptism for Yago Darby John Díaz.

"The John in that name is what he called his baptismal name, which is not traditionally added, of course, but he insisted."

Johnny takes the crinkling parchment into his hands. He sets it flat on the tabletop and runs his hands over its surface, traces Yago's long name. Yago? *Baptized?* He never even used God's name, except during sex. Never mentioned him in any late-night conversation. He was an agnostic as far as Johnny could tell. And if he was dragged along to Mass on a Sunday—usually because Angelo begged him to come—he would appear bored and bite his nails or count his change.

"Why in God's name would Yago want to be baptized and why in *your* church?" Johnny asks.

"As I told you, he was in distress, very lost. I believe this baptism gave him a feeling of inclusion. And John, you must know that many homosexual men and women embrace Catholicism," the priest informs him.

"But the church does not hug them back," Johnny says. He looks hard at the document before him. "Tell me, Father. Would you have baptized Yago if he had *not* been celibate? That's a tough question, isn't it? Would you?"

"That is not the situation I faced."

"Non-answer! C'mon, tell me! You're a priest so you'd better not lie."

"In the eyes of the Church, sexual..." and here he struggles to find the appropriate word, "interaction of one man with another would put Yago's soul into a sinful state. We believe that all souls carry original sin and that the sacrament of baptism cleanses that sin. The laws inherent in the commandments, in the Bible, and as interpreted by his Holiness are quite clear. I have sworn to obey those holy dictums."

"For once, Father, answer the question. Would you have baptized my husband if he was not practicing celibacy?"

"Then let me finish, John. I also believe that every priest in his interactions with both the faithful and nonbelievers acts as an instrument of God's will. So, given everything else your husband told me was true, then yes, I would have baptized him even if he were not celibate. I personally believe that love should be judged not on who you love, but how well you love."

Johnny closes his eyes, not wanting to cry in front of this man. He remembers Yago that last night, the secondhand black suit, the white shirt, and, painfully, those strands of silver in his hair.

"I can't tell you how much I miss him, Father. I wake up in the morning and hold his pillow next to my body. I don't know how I can ever wash that pillowcase. I haven't removed a single thing of his. I can't bring myself to go to the laundromat. I'd have to touch all his clothing, put it back in his drawers. How ridiculous."

Then Johnny does break down and Father Guyton reaches across the table and lays his hands on Johnny's arms. "Only time will make any of this bearable," he tells him. "Not better. Only bearable. Keep talking about it, Johnny. Share it with others who loved him."

Johnny looks up and wipes his eyes with the back of his hands like a little boy. "Tell me, Father, did he believe in an afterlife? Did you talk about that?"

"When he first came to me months ago, I can say that he had no faith. None to lose and none to find. He was starting from scratch. It felt like coming to me was his last straw. I stupidly told him that you can't come to God because you've exhausted all the other options. Because, of course, Johnny, that is the perfect time.

"He was often pugnacious in our discussions. Often cynical. But he listened to every word I said and often returned the next week with more questions. I do remember he asked about heaven; he was skeptical about its existence. I can say with conviction that on the day of his leaving me, on the day of his baptism, which was also Ash Wednesday, he believed in God, truly believed that he was worthy of God's love."

"Father, he died on Ash Wednesday. They found him on the street in the Village, badly cut and bruised in the face and body. I guess a fall following an alleged heart attack. I know very little about how and where he died."

"What street? On what street did they find him?"

"I'm sorry. I don't know that. I'm sure it's in some police report. When I saw him at the hospital, he was already long gone."

"What time of day? Roughly," Father Guyton asks.

"My guess, around nine at night."

The priest runs his fingers through his hair, giving him a bit of a pompadour. "I know this is an awkward request, especially coming from me, but could I trouble you for a glass of wine?"

Johnny smiles, goes over to the cabinet and selects a bottle, corkscrew, and two glasses. "I think the Lord preferred red, yes?"

"As do I," the priest answers.

Johnny opens the bottle and pours.

"Let me tell you just one thing more," Father Guyton says. "After I baptized him right there in my study, right before he went out into that raw night air, he asked me to give him ashes. He seemed very interested in ritual. I went back into the sanctuary and got the ashes while he waited there. Then I pushed back his hair and made the sign of the cross on his forehead with the ashes. 'Remember man that you are dust and unto dust you shall return.' I said those words, embraced him, tightened his beautiful red scarf around his neck, and he left."

Both men take a full mouthful of wine.

"But he is not dust, Johnny. Only his physical body failed him, not his soul. He was preparing his soul for passage. When I look back on it now, I think he did know what was coming. I really do."

"I can't remember if I kissed him before he left." Johnny recalls the red scarf that Angelo had given Yago, but not a kiss goodbye. "It bothers me not knowing. I can't remember if I did that evening."

"You did," Angelo says as he pulls the door open wide enough for him to slide through. "I saw you kiss Papa. You did."

"Thank you, son. Thank you for remembering for me."

Angelo walks over to the priest and stands straight-backed before him. The priest cups the boy's chin in his hand and examines his face. "I pray you were not in a fight."

Angelo beams. "I was! And you shoulda seen the other guy."

"Angelo! Tell Father the truth," Johnny says, pulling the boy towards him.

"Grandpa Darby threw this guy so far he dropped his beer bottle and it broke and cut my face. There was blood everywhere!"

"Oh…Darby. I've heard a lot about him," Father Guyton says.

"Yes, the legendary Darby," Johnny adds. "So many tales about Darby. Some are truth, more are fiction. Allyssa!" he shouts to the kitchen. "Four bowls of risotto and whatever salad you've concocted for the only diners in the joint." Then to Angelo, "Please, let's have no more talk of Abraham Darby."

CHAPTER SEVENTEEN • EGG WHITE
Weeks Later

THROUGH THE PASSING WEEKS DARBY HAS LABORED, NOT as an artist entangled in high emotion or intellectual pursuit, but more as a plumber or an electrician labors when confronted with what does not work and must construct in his mind what will. No music plays. There are only sirens, horns, and the sporadic, muffled grunts of truck traffic below.

He doesn't paint portraits of Yago or any living, feeling thing. He paints first an egg, an object seeming at first glance to be pure and perfect in shape. But Darby dissects the image, finds the asymmetry, the rough surface, its origins, the nonreflectance of the shell. He paints it in the center of a black velvet box, as though it were valuable.

His next effort is a huge canvas that depicts the soft-edged shapes beyond his fogged bathroom window. Then the following day, two more complex and meaningless works—the none too appealing contents of his refrigerator and a pile of his dirty clothes. On the next day, he daringly paints the black dress, thrown across his unmade bed. This is the very same dress worn by Sarah, reclaimed by Alejandra, and then transported like war booty by Darby back to Tribeca. This painting takes him a good part of his day, so he calls for his dinner, eats it, and drinks himself to sleep.

The next morning he ventures out, purchases a television on Canal Street, but never calls the cable company for service. No painting on that dark day.

He calls no one and no one attempts to reach him. There is mail delivered, but he rarely bothers to collect it.

More time passes like this. Twin paintings of the surface of his empty wooden table appear—one with the morning sun across it and the other at sunset. Where he once felt like a lion in his life, virile and productive, he is now more the sacrificial lamb, waiting out the obvious outcome. But he paints on, and there are soon dozens of elaborate depictions of anything he stumbles across without leaving his loft.

Then there is the problem of the Manning Gallery. Another exhibition is scheduled for July and he dreads facing the overly supportive curator. He can't recall her annoying name, perhaps something like April or June. But there is no new work, unless they are enamored with eggs and rotting food. Wait, he thinks. Maybe there is a way to sell these empty paintings. They could title it, "Grief: A Retrospective." They'll probably eat it up. Loss is so romantic and intoxicating when it's not yours.

He continues to paint even more pointless images, laughing at those who will seek to find meaning in them. After nearly a week of this, he stops and for days he does not paint. Darby leaves his loft early in the morning as the sun rises and walks along the Hudson River on the promenade that extends for miles north and south. Dodging speeding bicyclists and distracted tourists, he watches the straining motion of the river but does not see the daffodils or budding shrubs. The constant and aimless walking soon loses its numbing effect and he stops this, too.

But what is left to paint? He finds take-out containers and renders their white, cardboard flaps like the flying wings of a cornette atop a Polish nun.

Darby knows this brooding emptiness will drive him, not to a dark creative brilliance, but to insanity.

Then, a breakthrough. At nightfall, by the light of a bare bulb overhead, he paints his own reflection in the mirror above the bathroom sink. He's thoroughly drunk when he paints this and painfully sober the next morning when he appraises his work. Here is a wrecked man, a pathetic assemblage of slackened features, empty eyes, and something much, much darker. Rivers of white hair travel down his face like greasy icicles. His mouth hangs open almost in wordless surprise and what you see of his chest is hollowed in with shoulders slightly forward. He has painted his corpse, he thinks, or at least some being detached from life.

Throughout the following morning, his emptiness does ease at times, but it always returns, like hunger or fatigue. When it does lighten, he finds the simple emotion of missing his son.

Of course, he often did miss his son in the past, especially when Yago was nine or ten and travelling so extensively with Alejandra. After that, he rarely saw him and the times he did were awkward. But through the years that followed, Darby knew he walked the planet, this son, a father's foil against death, part of him that would continue on in the lovely genetic chain that was life. How broken that chain seems to be now, as he sits alone at an empty table in the center of his disheveled loft. It is now 2:13 on the afternoon of April 2nd, the day Yago would have been 39.

He presses his fists into his eyes, sees the small boy coated in fine sand, smells the salt in his wet hair, feels the terror raging through his own heart at the thought of losing him so many years ago. And now, he has.

Losing him. Too big to paint. Impossible to absorb.

He's breathing now in sharp gasps. Something heavy sits on his chest. Frightened, he finds his bed, brings the covers over his head, and sleeps for fifteen hours.

When he wakes there are hints of dawn. He feels strength, *but what to do with it?*

Darby stores away the paintings of nothing, and brings out many paintings of Yago to one long wall. He can see the perfect execution and the style that is his own. But not one is Yago—not his lush essence—and the painter's shortcomings become more evident as the boy grows into manhood.

He sees that he has always painted a posed, fixed figure. Painting photographs and illusions. All poses frozen in time. He feels that every one of these portraits is a fraud. Maybe his self-portrait in the bathroom mirror is his only success.

Then he comforts himself. *Isn't that true of any portrait painter? How can an artist capture more than gesture or expression, no matter how talented?* A painter has only limited abilities when tackling time.

He recalls another image, not his, but Alejandra's, that is somewhere in this loft. *What did she see and feel? What of that did she convey through her portraits?* He had a small watercolor from a series she did of Yago as a young boy on the beach in Costa Rica. She refused to sell them but gave one to Darby on his 50th birthday. Another hangs in Orient and the third had been given, of course, to Yago. She kept none for herself because, he clearly remembers her saying, "He is in my heart always." *But where is this watercolor?* Darby has not seen it in years. He searches through boxes of drawings, heavy covered folders with elegant ribbons tying them closed, and expensive archival cases, but can't find it.

Then he remembers. *The envelope!* It's in the wide drawer of his ancient oak desk, where he had tucked it away with the stack of drawings his son had done, the envelope he has seen so many times but rarely opened. The very envelope on which the young Yago had written:

FAMILY VALUBLES

—a label as endearing in its misspelling as in the carefully executed block printing.

Darby finds the envelope but is somehow certain that it is unwise to open this on his own, being the lamb and no longer the lion. Help is needed and he realizes who the perfect person to help him might be, if he dare ask.

Darby showers, puts on coffee. He will head out later for supplies, the basics, pizza, a pint, more paint.

‡ ‡ ‡

"Did Johnny send you?" He initially had not recognized the young woman who pried the pizza box from his hands in the chaos of Canal Street.

"C'mon, let me help you," Allyssa tells him. Darby has a bottle and three bulging plastic bags.

"Johnny told me where you live, but I came on my own. Just checking on you."

"Really? After all this time, someone wonders if I'm still alive?"

"Darby, don't be so dramatic. You know we've all been through some changes," Allyssa says, falling into step with him.

Some changes? Losing a son is some changes? "I'm fine. I just want to be left alone," Darby tells her, picking up his pace, hoping to lose her.

"I have something to ask you. Would you mind if I came up for just a few minutes?"

"Whatever you want to ask me, you can ask me here."

"Ten minutes," she pleads, a little flirtatiously.

He doesn't respond. Allyssa takes this as an invitation.

The loft space has a musty smell she can't quite identify, but assumes it's coming from the mound of dishes in the sink. Paintings are everywhere and especially strange is the line of portraits along one wall.

"Are those all Yago?" she asks.

No reply.

Darby gets two paper plates and places a triangle of pizza on each. It is the style of pizza favored by the indecisive…everything is on it. They eat standing and then he hands her a beer from the refrigerator. He grabs a second slice but she waves off another.

"What is it you want?" He is more abrupt than he intends. She is a sweet, vulnerable thing and does seem uncomfortable.

She sits at the table. "Johnny would never ask you for help and he wouldn't approve of me asking you."

"It's money, isn't it?"

"The funeral costs. They were huge and he doesn't have the money. There are hospital bills, too. And the restaurant following the service was a small fortune. Everyone is demanding to be paid. Dying is not cheap."

He puts down his paper plate, walks to the windows overlooking White Street. He feels a fiery ball of anger rising from his chest, burning his throat. "How much?"

"Whatever you can spare would help."

"I forgot your name."

"It's Allyssa. We've met. A zillion times."

He walks back to her. "Allyssa, I'm sure you know I'm pretty well off. That's why you're here."

She really is a beautiful girl. He sees where the boy gets his angelic looks, the golden curls, big eyes, pouty lips.

Allyssa knows he is appraising her; she is used to that. She smiles coyly, moves closer, takes his hand.

"You're kidding me!" Darby steps back. This creature has just leveled the playing field. He knows nothing about her other than that she is the boy's biological mother. The father he knows is Johnny, his son's lover. All reason enough to bolt. But here she is, actually unbuttoning her pretty gauze blouse, not taking her eyes off him.

He falls back into a wooden chair and amazingly, there she stands between his legs. Her bare, small but lovely breasts are about eye level. She touches the back of his head, not pulling her towards him, simply playing with his hair.

It is wonderful just to *feel* again. He thrills at the bulge in his trousers, the sudden dryness in his mouth, the way his heart thuds unevenly in his chest. Maybe the lion is poking his head from the den.

"You're a man, I'm a woman. No one else will know what happens in the next 30 minutes."

She smells of youth, like heavy fruit fallen too soon to the ground, earthy and sweet. On their own, his hands lift her long skirt, cup the tight mounds of her buttocks, and pull her to him.

Oh yes, he wants to be with her, to be inside her, to have her devour him, all his fear, the past weeks, the emptiness. And looking at her, he sees she has the confidence to do it. And the will.

But then, most unfortunately, he remembers the money.

"How much will this cost me, my dear?" he whispers.

It probably wasn't the mention of money that broke the spell, but the "my dear." No woman her age, he realizes too late, is going to go to bed with a man his age who calls her that. She backs away, now appearing shy and a little embarrassed.

"It's not that. I've always found you sexy, like in that older guy kind of way. But you were Yago's father and that seemed wrong."

"I am still Yago's father." Darby picks up Allyssa's blouse and hands it to her.

"I thought we were having a moment," she says as she dresses.

"I believe in a moment, but I'm old enough to also know that moments are linked, and there comes the moment after. And don't tell me it isn't about the money."

"You're calling me a whore?"

"But for a good cause. It's rather sweet, to think of a girl giving her body to honor the dead. Give me a number."

"Five thousand." She looks to him about twelve years old, caught out after her curfew.

Darby goes over to his desk and writes a check to Johnny for ten thousand. "I don't remember his last name. You fill it in." He lays it on the table and sits.

"Now tell me something about him, about Yago. Anything. You lived with them, didn't you? Tell me about him."

Allyssa sits directly across from him. "Like what?" To her credit, she doesn't look at the number on the check.

"It doesn't matter. Something endearing. There's so much I don't know."

"I can tell you that I had a huge crush on him. Pretty pointless, right? Can't help who you're attracted to. Anyway, that meant that just about everything he did was endearing to me. I loved dancing with him. He was an *amazing* dancer."

"Hmm."

"You like to dance?"

"Not at all," Darby says. "Too self-conscious. Look at me. Do I look light on my feet?"

She smiles. "Yago said that it was essential that a person dance at least once every day. He would dance around the kitchen…I don't think you've ever seen it, but the kitchen is really small. He'd grab one of us and make us dance with him. Didn't matter what music was playing. Johnny loves opera, which Yago detested. Said it was depressing. But he could even dance to opera! Kind of a silly, exaggerated ballet style. Hilarious."

He rises and throws away the pizza and its box, the plates, and beer bottles. "Tell me something else about him."

"He could be just as sad. Stay in bed all day. Wouldn't give you more than two-word answers. 'You hungry?' 'Not really.' 'Want company?' 'I'm good.'

"And then it would lift and he wouldn't shut up. He was all lovey and fun again. Johnny called it whites and yokes. Code, you know. Whites was when Yago was all clear and jiggly and fine. Johnny would warn me and Angelo if he turned the other way. 'Beware! Yokes!' If it was a really bad spell, it was 'Look out! Hard-boiled yokes.'"

"Hmm." Again.

"Are you like that? Does he get that from you?"

Darby realizes that he hasn't had an actual conversation with anyone in weeks. "Well, I'm yokes most of the time. Better disposition for a painter. Now Alejandra…definitely whites."

"Oh yeah. I just love her."

"A common malady."

"Yago adored her, of course. He was always whites when she was around. Moped for days after she left."

"Got anything else?" Darby doesn't want to hear about his superior parenting half.

"He loved to eat. Hated exercise, like running to nowhere or going to a gym. Thought it was silly. He wasn't much of a drinker. His tolerance was so low and he didn't like to be laughed at. He hated that, was really hurt by being ridiculed or teased. Took things personally."

"As for alcohol, I have the tolerance of an offshore barge," Darby says. "Makes drinking very expensive. I don't know if I take things personally. I really don't think about what other people think of me. My work, yes. But not me personally."

Allyssa slips on her little silver flats. "I gotta go. We really appreciate the help."

"Why wouldn't I want to pay for my son's funeral?"

"You know you can come around if you want to. Angelo thinks you're some powerful mythic figure."

"I don't think so."

"Is there something else you want to ask me…about Yago?"

"Another time." There is already so much for him to digest.

Allyssa persists. "Don't you want to know what he thought of you?"

"I know what he thought of me."

"Do you? He talked about you a lot and once he got started…especially to Angelo…"

"It's okay. I don't need to know what he said," Darby says.

"You'd be surprised, I bet."

"Allyssa!" he warns.

"So you don't need to know about the book he made of all the random sketches you did of him, on menus, paper bags, whatever." She's spitting this out quickly. "He saved them all. You flip through the pages and you can almost see him grow up.

"He has another scrapbook of articles written about you, reviews of shows, postcards from the exhibitions. He and Angelo have kept that up. Have the people at the Manning told you how often they've seen him there, staring at himself through your eyes? Staring at all your work there, seeing the world as you see it?"

He glares at her. *How could he possibly know these things?*

"I failed with Yago. I knew how to love him as a boy. I didn't know how to love him as a man."

"I gotta go, Darby. Let it go. You did what you could." Allyssa snatches the check and scurries off.

Alone, he is lost and aimless. *What is next?* There, open like a gaping wound, is the pizza box crammed into the waste bin. Tempting, but he will not paint it.

He does not want to drink or sleep, but he's buzzing with something, some frenetic energy demanding release, a wire stretched too tight, ready to snap. An urge, almost sexual, a definite need.

So he paints, not from photographs, not from memory, but from necessity. It is the one painting that must emerge if he is to survive his loss and his guilt.

It is of Yago, of course.

Yago, sensual, vulnerable, playful, and searching. Yago's eyes locked with the artist's. His son, loved as he was, loving as he was. Here painted with the addition of wings. Not an angel's. A bird's.

A painting born not from love, but of love, uniting what is most fragile with what is most powerful.

When the work is finished, it is well into the night. Darby is weak but elated. Hungry now, he thinks he should go out, have a sit-down meal in a restaurant, but he's afraid to leave the painting. He's afraid that it's not real, that it might be gone when he returns.

He brings the large painting near him, leaning it against the back of a chair. Darby sits with it, feeling both a connection with his son and the willingness to let him go. It is the first moment of simple happiness he has enjoyed in a very long time. He breathes in the silence of the open room, the precious silence that sometimes falls on Manhattan for long moments in the middle of the night.

Darby stares at the table's surface, illuminated by a single lamp. He examines the irregular gaps between the wide planks and the hard matter trapped in each long crevice. That matter is composed of crumbs from past meals, dust, sweat mixed with linseed oil, and spilled wine. Could a bit of a younger Yago's lunch be lodged there or perhaps a drop of wine from that rare glass they might have shared years later? *What of his son is still here? What of him resides within his father?*

Yago wasn't buried in a box in the ground as Johnny had wanted, as in a place to primp and place flowers. Yago was cremated, the only thing Darby requested concerning the entire post-life process. But to his profound horror, Johnny informed him that the ashes of his son were to be passed out like party favors. He imagined the tightly rolled, little baggies of his son's remains which would be delivered to a few close friends and significant locations. Some would be emptied into the air just above Sheridan Square (and likely into the exhaust fumes of downtown traffic on Seventh Avenue), some of Yago would be placed in a pig-shaped cookie jar on Court Street, and some mailed to Escazú. Darby had been promised his own stash and received it not long ago, arriving via the U.S. Postal Service without insurance or return receipt. He had known its contents without opening the recycled box and had stashed it in a kitchen cupboard next to phone books and his collection of flashlights.

He retrieves the box and places it before him on the table. It is surprisingly light in weight for such a sacred thing. He shakes it and a solid mass inside moves back and forth. He rips the packing tape and opens the flaps. Inside he finds crumpled newspaper to cushion Yago's ride through Brooklyn and into Lower Manhattan. And below that, there is a bulging leather wallet and his baggie of ashes. He holds the baggie in his hands briefly and then drops it to the floor. He stares at it for a long time. When he finally picks it up, he holds it gingerly, then unrolls his son's plastic casket and lays it flat on the table.

The contents are the same color as Yago's skin in winter, a creamy pale gold—a coincidence. He pushes the fine powder in all directions. He discovers larger fragments, perhaps the bones that composed his son's tall, elegant frame or perhaps his perfect teeth. The corporal essence is hard to discern once the tissues, the blood, the hair, the heart that failed have all been reduced to something like what he'd shovel out of his woodstove.

Darby shakes its contents to the bottom and carefully opens the baggie. It feels sacrilegious, but still he takes a pinch of the ashes and rolls it between his fingers. He thought it would be silkier, but finds it more like a mixture of coarse and fine sand. However, when he drops it back into the baggie, there is a residue on his fingertips that will not rub off. He tries to brush it back into the bag, but to no avail. The residual fine powder does have a silkiness after all and it coats his skin, entering his own body through fine pores.

He takes the wallet that accompanied the ashes. How intimate the curving form and the reassuring scent of old leather. His hands travel as his son's had, revealing a driver's license with a very serious Yago in his official portrait, as well as his height and eye color. *How could one word describe the colors in his eyes?* Glints of his mother's green, and from him, a buried blue that can only be seen in the brightest sunlight, all blended in a sea of gold.

Following the license in foggy sleeves are a few photographs of Angelo, Johnny, and two very flattering shots of a youthful Alejandra. The last sleeve is reserved for his father, a grainy black and white picture on newsprint. It undoubtedly accompanied some article about him or his work. Darby takes that image from the sleeve and finds it brittle and old, much as he feels right now. It's an odd addition to Yago's miniature family album, but at least he is included.

In the wallet's folding money area, Darby counts 17 twenties. Impressive but surprising for a man that barely got by and had no real occupation or ambition. Behind the bills—Yago being a good samaritan—is a Trojan lubricated condom in a flashy aqua foil package that was wrinkled and weathered.

Tucked into little pockets of the wallet are two credit cards (both in Johnny's name), a Starbucks gift card, a GMHC identification card, and one holy card. On the front of that is an illustration of

St. Joseph, the trusting father of all fathers. On the reverse is the name, address, and the personnel (including the webmaster) of a Catholic church on Sixth Avenue.

Darby closes the wallet and cups it with both hands. His earlier sense of connection with his son feels not stronger nor diminished. It lingers comfortably. It's death that puzzles him, the way it is so poorly integrated into life, as though being shunned and unwelcomed, it must loiter until it forces its way in. He thinks of corpses burning on pyres in the Ganges River. He sees the cemetery in Queens where both his parents are buried, the cemetery he thinks looks like a mini-Manhattan with its streets of towering tombstones. This is a cemetery he hasn't visited since both were laid to rest. *Laid to rest?* More denial.

Where does his son rest? On this table in a sandwich bag? In cupboards and cookie jars? On a bench in Sheridan Square under some stranger's ass?

He knows a better place.

Darby carries his last painting of Yago back into the studio area of his loft and loads it onto the easel with the adaptable mast, so that the canvas can dry flat later. He brings two flood lamps to shine additional light on the glossy, wet surface and stares deeply into the golden green eyes he created. They are now face to face, man to man, father to son.

He creates a new palette, and applying titanium white, Payne's gray, ivory black, a small amount of cerulean blue. Then onto Darby's mother's glass pie dish, the artist mixes a generous amount of yellow ochre and Prussian blue, and then empties the baggie containing Yago's remains into the paint.

With a new palette knife, he swirls the ashes into the paint, then adds his own special blend of linseed oil, Damar varnish, and turpentine. Darby selects a Lexington Flat and begins to fold the richly textured medium and new colors into the wings that caress Yago's torso. The father is creating wings that can be wrapped around his son like a protective cloak or utilized for flight. The new medium adds a three-dimensionality that evokes wind and motion. And without the artist's intent, the coloring of these wings mirrors the complex palette of Yago's eyes.

Darby takes a great deal of time in the use of this special paint, lovingly applying it with both palette knife and brush, perfecting each feather and its integration into the wing. There are many ways to bury the dead, to return their bodies to the eventual dust they must become. This solemn burial in paint is a perfect send-off for them both.

Darby is aware of problems, both chemical and archival, that may evolve by adding his son's ashes to the paint. They will likely affect the color and integrity of the painting over time. But those, to him, are advantages in this particular work.

Hours later, he is finished and stands back from the painting. "This is you, Yago, for me," he tells the painting. "Away! Away you fly." Here, in one of his most intimate moments with his son, Darby releases him and all of his own expectations, illusions, misconceptions, and needs. Yago was a man, only a man, not his father's dream of a man, not any image of a man created in the imagination of an artist.

He was simply Yago, and that was more than sufficient for those who loved him. And he knows now, there were many.

Darby sheds the emptiness that has been his companion for weeks. Sunlight pours into the loft and he takes his jacket to go out, not knowing the temperature or even the day of the week.

His left hand is flat against the cold metal door and his right hand is wrapped around the doorknob when he freezes in place. A shaking begins in his neck, then bolts down his spine until his whole body is quaking with a near-seizure intensity. He becomes desperately cold and then quickly feverish.

He hears movement on the other side of the door, an impatient shuffling of feet, then faint laughter and mumbling in a small familiar voice.

The door grows so hot that Darby must back away. He puts his jacket over the searing doorknob and opens it, but exposes no spirit, living or not. There is no one in the hall, but he thinks there must have been. He can feel an emotion still present, an odd but very real sensation. Like one might feel at the scene of an accident or during the mass singing of an anthem.

He races down the metal stairs to street level. His heart is pounding when he swings the door open onto White Street, where the sun is washing over from Sixth Avenue and the seasons have changed.

Before him stands a small child in his Sunday clothes, holding in his hands a stuffed penguin, a chocolate bunny, and what looks like a handmade book.

"Why wouldn't you let me in?" Angelo says.

"You alright, Abe?" Johnny asks from behind him.

"I don't know. What is alright?" Darby whispers.

"My personal goal lately," Johnny answers.

"How did you get here?" Darby suspects a modicum of divine intervention.

"Ah, F to the A," Johnny says.

Darby stares back at the boy, who has lowered his head as if he's misbehaved.

"Sorry, Abe. I know it's early," Johnny explains. "Got to get to work. Brunch is big for us today. I wanted to thank you for helping us out...with the check. We really appreciate it."

"So then, is it Sunday?"

"All day." Johnny takes a step closer, but stops. His finds Darby's appearance unsettling. He hasn't shaved in who knows how long and there's paint on his hands, his clothes, even his face. "Did you get the ashes, Darby?"

Darby looks at his hands. There are still oils and ashes clinging to his fingers, on the back of his hands. "Yes. I buried them."

"We put Papa in the cookie jar," Angelo announces. "Allyssa says the cookies can't be in there anymore. I think Papa would like them."

"I know, your father told me that would be his final resting place in your home," Darby says. The vulnerability in Angelo pains him. He lowers himself to his knees, then sits on his heels directly in front of the boy. Darby points to the book and stuffed animal that Angelo holds.

"I've met your penguin, but what is this book you have?" Darby asks.

"These are pictures you made of Papa. He made a book. Daddy said you might want it." Angelo hands the book to Darby.

It's a scrapbook, the type with the padded covers and gold curlicues. Darby realizes that this is the book Allyssa referred to, and yes, inside are the scraps of paper and bags and menus. Every sketch is simple and sweet. Like his boy. Like this boy.

Darby closes the book and places his hand on Angelo's cheek. "Don't you want them?"

Angelo looks uncomfortable, but is honest. "Yes."

"Then you should keep them." Darby rises slowly to his feet. "Is there anything else?" There is a surprising tenderness in his question.

"Are you mad at me?" Angelo asks Darby.

"Why would I be?"

"I remind you of Papa."

Darby briefly closes his eyes, exhales heavily. "That's a good thing, Angelo."

"C'mon, my little man. Gotta get back to the bacon," Johnny says and puts his hand on Darby's shoulder. "You should come around sometime. We're not blood family, but family by choice can sometimes be even better than family by chance. You know what I mean?" Then he delivers a little wink that Darby has always found incredibly annoying.

"Maybe. What Sunday is this exactly?" Darby asks.

When Johnny tells him that it's Easter Sunday, Darby remembers that he must shower and get on the uptown train. Even though his calendar is still showing February, he had circled this day in April much earlier in a rare, fleeting moment of optimism.

CHAPTER EIGHTEEN • GESSO ON CANVAS

Later That Morning

THERE ON THE MESSAGE BOARD ON THE FRONT OF THE church, solemnly encased in glass, are the two words that have made this at all possible. The two words that both laugh in her face and yet make her credible. Two words she can fess up to. That can make her absence forgivable and her return permissible. They connote not an excuse but a process. *On Doubt.*

Weeks after returning to her own baffling life, she had experienced a dream. In the dream she inhabits the luscious wash of Costa Rican landscape from Alejandra's watercolor in the Orient living room. She can feel the fluid heat and sensuous sand that squeezes pleasantly between her toes. The sound of the water is that of a small cat drinking from a shallow bowl. Colors seep into her skin and she feels totally relaxed, almost euphoric.

Then another figure approaches in the same hesitating though purposeful saunter as an earlier midwinter visitor. Now as a boy—the boy painted in his mother's imagination—Yago comes closer. As in the watercolor, he is translucent but for his heavy wet curls. He is innocent, happy, and carefree.

Yago extends his hand for hers. She takes it and with her free hand touches his hair and then his downy cheek. *To be a child is to be exactly as this, confident in the natural world, loving and lovable.*

It begins to rain although the sky is cloudless. They share their thoughts without words.

Then in the distance through the tender, sun-filled rain, they see Alejandra walking towards them along the shoreline, her lovely, full skirt of many colors trailing in the sea water. Both Sarah's and the boy's hearts fill with longing and it intensifies painfully as she nears them.

Alejandra pulls the boy into her arms and then places her palm on Sarah's shoulder. "We should say a prayer of gratitude for all of this, don't you think?" says the artist who created this lush world. Then without a moment's passing, mother and son are swimming like dolphins, naked shimmering creatures who leap above the water's surface in impossible arcs, blending like watercolors in the misty air.

Sarah remains planted in the sand, aching to but unable to join them. She watches them swim further from shore, and soon the two are tiny glittering dots on the horizon and Sarah is alone, full of fear for their safety, heavy with shame for her hesitating, doubting nature.

In this confusion, she woke from the dream, still alone in her double bed with only the nascent dawn to comfort her. She frantically left her bed and traveled through her small apartment, turning on every light she passed until she reached the kitchen table. There in pencil on a paper bag, she wrote about that paralyzing doubting she experienced in her dream. This would become the heart of the sermon in her one-Sunday performance, to be delivered at the imposing church on West 139th Street. This on the Sunday of all liturgical Sundays, the day Christ rose from the dead. On this day to shatter all human doubting, she would reveal her own:

Doubts about her adequacy, about her ability to protect whom she loves and doubts that she, too, will be protected by those who love her. And larger, deeper doubts, those that enchain us all as human beings, about the sustainability of love, of trust, of faith.

The text of the sermon flew out of her like an exorcism. Although she was tempted to equate doubt with fear, she did not. She was tempted to assign to doubt intellectual curiosity, but rejected that as well. It was simply human frailty. And, most importantly, it was a waste of energy and a massive roadblock to the recovery of faith.

In the eventual delivery of her sermon that Easter morning, she stuck to the words she'd written about her travels through the dark passages of her own doubting. She spoke generally about her separation from her husband without naming why it had occurred. She detailed her wanderings after Ash Wednesday with thinly veiled references to sex (prompting uncomfortable readjustments to seating postures in the congregation) and other overindulgences, including alcohol and food. She spoke about what she remembered from her magical but baffling dream. She credited Alejandra for opening her eyes to her own sensual nature. She thanked Alexander for his listening and his well-intentioned instructions. Then, more shocking to them than the fact that their associate pastor had enjoyed extramarital sex, was the telling of her encounter with a seductive apparition on that predawn winter beach. She spoke about Yago, that boy in her dream now a grown man. She added all the bizarre details she could recall, including his mockery, his insight, his sensuality, even the bird with the playing card in its beak.

In closing, she apologized for all the questions she had thrown at them in her previous sermon months prior. She announced that what she had just shared contained the answers to her doubts. Answers they would have to decipher, that they should continue to decipher in their own lives. The clues were buried, she acknowledged, but they were there. They always are. Have faith, she had told them, that God will send a person, a painting, even a dark angel to guide them. Be aware! Blessed be. Amen.

She had delivered an odd message for Easter Sunday, but then, she felt it was most appropriate to talk about beginning life again.

Now the Reverend Sarah Obadias stands at the front doors of the church and politely shakes the hands of her congregation. No one mentions anything about the specifics of her revelations. A few say they are glad she's back and hope she feels better. She knows the sermon was given more for her sake than theirs, so she is not offended by their bland niceties.

The last hand she holds in hers is Darby's.

She looks at him with a curious amazement. *Where was he hiding?* How could she have missed that blazing white hair and pale face among her congregants?

"I think you mentioned us in a less than positive light," he says. "Like an illness looking for a cure."

"*Us?*" the reverend asks.

"How about 'Nice to see you, Darby'?"

"I'm surprised to see you."

"I see that. Johnny has invited us to dinner," he lies. He hasn't talked to Johnny since the episode outside his building this morning. The invitation had been vague and open-ended.

"There's that *us* again."

"Yes, you and me. Dinner. In Brooklyn," he emphasizes, as if the location explains it all.

Sarah lowers her head and raises the silk stole from her shoulders. No comment.

"I liked your sermon. I think I might even go to church once in a while if I thought I'd hear that kind of honesty," Darby admits.

She examines him, but fears he could mistake that for real concern, as though she might care whether or not he goes to church. Like he might be her next convert. She sees that he has shaven though not with great accuracy, and that he has washed and combed his hair.

Still, his clothes are too wintery for this mild April morning and the stench of alcohol escapes from every pore. But then again—much like the first time she saw him—there is that carnal yearning, an attraction now with a little history.

"I'm no theologian," he comments modestly, "but I think what you were talking about is connecting. You know, connecting your doubts with your faith, you with your God. Me with my son."

This does get her attention. From her sermon he has learned about the beach and the trickster with the playing cards. "You've had contact with Yago?" she asks.

"Not as phenomenal as between the two of you," Darby says. "Some communication, let's call it. Not my strong suit but I'm trying. I can feel him, sense his presence. I don't paint him anymore. Well, only once after he died…the way I experience him now."

In the days they had spent together, she never heard so many words fly so easily from his mouth. But then again, Yago had just died.

"Why are you here, Darby?"

"You were easy to find," he says as he brushes imagined bits of winter from the sleeves of his jacket. "I copied some of the contacts on your phone. Figured out your church and visited its website. I love that churches have websites. Soon even God will have one." He can't reveal the truth. Can't admit that he feels that she has somehow brought him closer to his son. That once he could feel again, he found he missed her.

"That's not what I asked. But thank you for returning my phone," she says more calmly. "I know you called my daughter. She checked with me before giving you my address."

"She wanted me to send it to her and she'd mail it to you. I refused. Told her that I wanted to include a very personal note. That settled it. She called me back with the information."

"I got no note."

"She was protective, understandably," he says. "But she knew about me, about us."

"Darby, please stop using the *us* word."

"Well, I think she assumed we'd slept together."

"That doesn't make us an *us*."

"What does that make us, Reverend Obadias?"

"Desperate?" She immediately regrets using that word. Sees how it stings him. He had lost his son. She had lost less.

Darby buttons up his corduroy jacket unnecessarily. "I'm not sure what you are accusing me of, or what I even want here. But, I'm here." Then, with more compassion, "Your husband? Is that it?"

"That is the past."

"So, join us for dinner."

"As if one follows the other! As if my being on my own permits me to have dinner with you. *My problem is you!* Your all-consuming life that devours everything in its path. I need time and space to figure out my *own* life."

"Dinner isn't until six." Another lie.

Sarah shakes her head disbelievingly. Darby looks like a boy on the verge of a whimpering tantrum should he not get his way. It's almost charming.

"Sarah, if it were all about me, I wouldn't have been sitting in that back pew."

"Just let me think about it. I am not promising I'll be there."

He searches through the musty index cards in his head. "Carroll Gardens, near the church we went to together. Court and Carroll Street, that's it."

‡ ‡ ‡

There's something in the hypnotic swaying of subway cars on their tracks that can lull a person into either lazy self-examination or sleep. But since Darby does not sleep on subways, he recounts the pleading lies he threw down for Sarah. He feels some pride in his cunning deceptions. The more disinterested she became, the more determined he was to lure her back into his life.

His vigor has returned and he wonders why. Executing the last painting of Yago had been a huge release. And he had recently shed the bulk of his aimless, lackluster works of low art. The Manning Gallery had sent a van to fetch them. He knew he looked a fright, but believed his lack of proper hygiene might add a needed seriousness and intent to his work.

And admit it or not, he had been excited to see the minister in action. There had been power in her words even if he could not decipher their exact meaning. It made him feel like he had been a part of something larger than himself.

As he grabs his worn, canvas satchel and hurries to his connecting train, he remembers the curator's call only this morning as he was rushing to get out and uptown. Did the woman even know it was Sunday, let alone Easter? She was desperate to talk with him about *the work*. Then, her voice hoarse with pity, out came all those wretched staid phrases of condolence. But when he had asked her if she'd ever met his son, she confirmed what Allyssa had said. She and the staff saw him often, and often with his son. Why, there were even bag lunches the two shared, so comfortable were they in the gallery. Of course, food was not allowed, but this was overlooked in their case. Then came the shocking statement that sometimes Yago brought other men there. Some of those men bought Darby's drawings, even paintings, often those of Yago. That's when he hung up the phone.

So it was true. How odd, Darby thinks now on the heaving, rocking F train as it screams through tunnels burrowed through rock, how odd that his son knew his father through the father's renderings of him. And that, sadly, the father knew his son in exactly the same way. Awash in art. Bankrupt in real emotion.

When Darby emerges from the Carroll Street station, it has rained and he is disoriented. He must, against his nature, ask for directions. He hasn't been to Johnny's restaurant in many years, not since he and Alejandra had put on a hugely entertaining display of their disjointed, constantly misfiring relationship. The theatrics culminated in a screaming match, each hurtling profanities (hers in Spanish) at each other to celebrate Yago's thirtieth birthday. Of course, there had been no Angelo yet and the place was called something innocuous like Seeds of the Future Bistro. *Seeds of the Future? Why not Pods of the Past?*

Darby himself never names his paintings for this very reason. He thinks that painters and chefs should hire poets or actual writers to name their precious works and establishments. Visual artists are not good writers; they don't think in words, so the titles of their works are often banal or tortuously obvious. All his paintings are named by the date they were completed, those dates clearly indicated on the back of the wood frame. Even that seems like too much. He believes that if it is not clear what the painting is about, no title for the work will make it any clearer. A brilliant title for a crappy painting still renders a crappy painting.

Darby vows to call the gallery tomorrow. He must be adamant in insisting that no titles be added, no aids given to their interpretation, no explanatory brochure. No pressed type on the white gallery walls, only his name will be allowed. And along with the ban on *Take-Out Container No. 3* and *Eulogy of the Egg*, there must also be no mention of the death of his son.

Darby finally has meandered his way to a park bench across the street from the restaurant. He sits behind an iron fence, which only seems to imprison harmless trees and cigarette butts within the borough park. He thereby acknowledges to himself just how little control he has once his paintings are out there. *Who can keep the overly empathetic curator or her staff from revealing to a reviewer or visitor the tragedy buried in the work, especially if that tragedy increases its value?*

Through the bars, he concentrates on the four cafe tables and chairs arranged on each side of the open double doors. It's a perfect early spring afternoon, comfortably warm. All the restaurant's outdoor tables are taken and littered with espresso cups, plates, and newspapers. At one table sits a solitary boy, Angelo, with a pad and pencils. As he draws and pauses to think, he pulls on his curls and waves his left hand excitedly before he continues to put on paper the image in his head. It is a combination of gestures reminiscent of Yago who, Darby realizes, has left his mark on this boy.

The lovely and dangerous Allyssa comes out and bends over Angelo. She smiles at the boy's masterpiece and messes with his hair. Minutes later, she returns with a sandwich nearly the size of Angelo's head. To Darby's combined horror and thrill, Allyssa looks across the street directly at him. She smiles and waves him over, then points to the sandwich, which is cut in two. She pokes the boy's shoulder and then he, too, looks over and waves excitedly, wiggling in his seat. Again, like Yago at that age.

Darby is confused as to what he should do. *It was them he came to see, especially the boy.* It would be cowardly to scamper away and crawl like a vole back into the subway. Still, his feet won't commit to any action so he stands and throws them a wave that looks unfortunately like a cartoonish "That's all Folks!"

Still, Allyssa's smile is sweet enough to charm the liver spots off his skin and he cannot refuse. He takes the long walk to the gated entrance and makes his way down Carroll. When he reaches the restaurant, Allyssa has left, but Angelo pats the seat of the chair on his right and returns to his drawing. It is as if this little shared luncheon was the most ordinary thing in the world, done often and without fanfare. Darby sits as instructed. He runs his finger over the boy's scar above his eye, just a thin, pink stroke of the finest brush on his perfect skin.

"Don't say I never gave you anything," Darby says.

The humor escapes Angelo. "Why would I say that?"

"The scar, remember?" Darby reminds him. "My gift to you."

"Girls like it," Angelo says, not looking up from his work.

An extra plate and two tall glasses of lemonade with tinkling ice arrive and a closer look at Allyssa. He's proud of his willpower with her yesterday, but, like any man, regrets it as well.

"I've invited Sarah for dinner. Here. At six," Darby says. "I doubt she'll come." *There, that's taken care of.*

"No problem," she says. "I'll just have Johnny call to remind her...or encourage her...whatever."

"Johnny call her? How would he do that?"

Allyssa looks baffled. "On her cell? You know, that new device that just came out."

"He has her number?"

"She gave it to him. In Orient. They talk, like every week, I guess. She came to dinner a couple weeks ago."

"I like her..." Angelo perks up.

"Angelo! Enough with the boobies!" Allyssa scolds. "He's just not used to seeing a woman blessed like that. Me and Alejandra, you know, not so much."

But Darby is barely listening. He's lost in the realization that during his weeks of hermitted depression, everybody else was sipping cappuccino and admiring the minister's anatomical gifts.

"Eat your sandwich, Darby," Allyssa scolds as if he were a misbehaving child. "Johnny's super busy, but I'm sure he'll create something really special if he knows Sarah's coming to dinner." She adds as she goes back inside, "And you, too, of course."

Angelo and Darby eat together in silence. The boy is having trouble with the girth of the sandwich, so Darby politely takes his plate. He disassembles the sandwich, cutting the bread, meat, cheese, and roasted red peppers into smaller pieces. He then forms a chain of these small bits that spirals from the center of the plate to its very edges. He's done this before.

Angelo's eyes light up. "Do I start in the middle or the outside?"

"That's a personal decision," Darby tells him. "You choose."

So the boy—quite creatively in Darby's opinion—begins at the center, but eats only every other piece, preserving the initial design.

Once they're finished, Darby pulls out the envelope from the satchel he had stashed beneath his chair. He hands it to Angelo.

"Family valubles," the boy reads. "Is it my family?"

It's a complicated question and Darby wants to answer honestly.

"Family by choice," he tells Angelo. "Always the best."

CHAPTER NINETEEN • SALSA VERDE

At Roughly the Same Time

*"Almighty God, unto whom all hearts are open,
all desires known, and from whom no secrets are hid..."*

The Book of Common Prayer

IT IS NO GREAT COINCIDENCE THAT WHILE WALKING BACK to her apartment after the service, that right on the same spot on West 125th Street, Sarah should come across the young man she had assaulted weeks before.

She sees him first. He is alone this time, leaning against a parking meter, reading. He is dressed much differently, in a pressed shirt and slacks. She knows she should leave the poor boy alone, is ashamed of her earlier behavior. But after the baffling sermon she had delivered and her equally confusing conversation with Darby, she can't just walk past him.

Sarah approaches from the side and lays her hand gently on his shoulder, but it spooks him. He pushes back her arm in defense.

"Sorry," Sarah says. "Again."

He looks at her with eyes narrowed. "I know you?"

"I'm pretty sure it was you I harassed…weeks ago," she tells him.

He rolls his eyes, looks away, returns to his book. But Sarah is determined in her quest for forgiveness. "I need to apologize. I never should have touched you."

He slams his book shut. "Listen, lady. You don't know anything about me, okay? If you need to feel better about roughing me up, fine. You can just feel better. I really don't give a…" He stops himself and starts walking away from her, throwing up a hand dismissively.

"Wait," she calls out. "Wait. Maybe I want to get to know you better. Learn something about you."

He turns. "Why?"

"Can't I just want to?" Sarah asks. "Just let me buy you lunch. Anywhere you like."

"You want to buy me lunch? So we can sit and chat? About what? All the things we ain't got in common?"

"You can order it to go. You don't have to talk to me," she says with just a speck of anger.

"Then you'll leave me alone?"

"Or I'll leave you alone right now."

He wasn't expecting that. "No, I could eat."

He points to a restaurant across the street called Como Bueno.

"That's fine. I love Spanish food."

"Yeah, everybody does. It's just those Spanish people they don't like so much."

Sarah senses that they both have a little work to do. When they enter the restaurant, a young woman asks if they want the main floor or downstairs. Sarah looks to her companion.

He doesn't answer right away. Looks at his watch. "I guess we can sit down and eat. It's nice downstairs."

A very small victory but Sarah is grateful. And once she sees the lower room, she's even more pleased. It looks like a little Mexican chapel. Against one exposed brick wall is an oblong table covered with statues of the Virgin Mary, as well as lit candles and various colored bottles. Just above the table is a lovely portrait of a very Spanish Madonna, whose framed image is adorned with masses of yellow, red, and blue flowers. Above that, a Mexican sombrero, red felt with gold embroidery, positioned as if the Mother of Jesus had just flung it celebratorily in the air.

All the dozen or so tables are covered with red linen and an impressive assortment of sauces, hot and hotter. The young woman seats them, even pulling out Sarah's chair for her.

In the dim light it's difficult for Sarah to read the menu, which is in Spanish. "Why don't you order for us?"

When he does order, she can read well enough to see that he's likely making selections from the right side of the menu where the prices are listed. It will be *pescado al coco, camarones enchilados,* and *bistec de palomilla,* all of her penance delivered in his perfect Spanish. Then a multitude of side dishes are ordered, from *tostones* to *ensalada mixta* and, of course, the *café con leche.*

"Well, you are hungry," Sarah comments. "Good."

"If it wasn't this, it would have been mac and cheese out of a box," he says.

"I like that, too." Why, she wonders, is she lying?

"Yeah, right. Your mac and cheese is probably some gourmet crap with fancy noodles and French cheeses."

"Lately, it's been Kraft." That, at least, is true.

Salad, fried plantains, and two plates arrive. As he arranges his food, she gets a chance to really look at him. He's a handsome boy, hair the texture of hers but longer, a little looser. A straight, regal nose and piercing, but playful eyes. Golden skin.

"Are you Guatemalan?" she asks while loading up her own plate.

"Puerto Rican and some of your people."

"Will you tell me your name?"

He lifts his head. "Are we chatting now?"

"Just your name and then we can eat."

"Fair enough. Rafael."

"Hebrew. And in Spanish, too. God has healed," she says.

"How do you know that?" he asks, showing little interest.

"Just something I studied. I'm Sarah, in case you're interested."

More food is brought to the table and they must bring another table over to accommodate it all. They eat in silence, as promised. She thinks she's been pushing too hard; resolves to lay back.

Despite their best efforts, much food is left on the tables. Rafael asks that it be wrapped up. He wants to take it home.

"Tell me a little about you, Rafael. What's your passion?" So much for laying back.

"My passion? That's a crazy question. Man, you're good. But I ain't gonna tell you. If I did, you'd know too much."

Sarah assesses her companion; perhaps he's softening a bit. He is at least talking. "What's wrong with that, me knowing you?"

"Gives you power."

"Over?" she asks.

"Me."

"Let me understand. Knowing what you're passionate about gives me power over you?"

"How can you not know that?" Rafael says. He stirs a mound of sugar into the *café con leche* just delivered.

"Not an answer," Sarah says, bolder now and growing impatient. "How does knowing what Rafael is passionate about empower Sarah?"

"Lady, you're persistent. I'll give you that. What a person is most passionate about is what he fears losing most. It makes him vulnerable to attack. But I'll tell you what. It's not what you think."

"Amazing. You know what I think."

Two large bags of leftover food and the check are placed on the nearby table. Sarah places a credit card on the check without even looking at it.

"Alright. I'm like this math wizard. It's so easy, like a game, a riddle to me. Science, too. I'm an all A student. Bet you didn't think that?"

"I didn't think you weren't," she says. "So that's your passion? Math and science?"

"Shit, no. I paint."

She wants to tell him that there are already too many painters in her life. *Couldn't it be something else?* "Go on. Tell me more."

"I'm really into Diego Rivera. You know who he is? He's like this crazy, Marxist, intense muralist. Painted people here in the thirties. He was all about the poor working stiff, how much of your fucking soul you have to portion off to get by."

"Tell me what you paint, Rafael."

"Murals, like my man, Diego. But he painted on panels made of metal and mortar. I use plywood, found stuff. Portable, like some of his, but way more so."

"What are they about, these murals you paint?" she asks.

"My life. My life here, like a diary," he says, and taking out his phone adds, "I'll show you one."

Even on the tiny rectangular screen, she can see the precision and heart he's put into the image. It's of a young man, probably him, with a large, open cloak around him. Huddled inside are women and children. "Beautiful, powerful," she tells him.

"I got plans," Rafael says. "Plans for me and Celeste. There's an art school in Miami my teacher told me about. We're going there when I finish school."

"Celeste? Who is Celeste? Your girlfriend?"

"You met her. Another misinterpretation on your part."

"The girl you were verbally abusing on the street?" Sarah asks.

"Yeah, I was breaking her down. I was!" His neck stretches across the table. "But you don't know why because you don't know who she is. She's my little sister, by eleven months. We're practically freakin' twins."

"But you were..."

"Pissed. You bet I was. She was getting messed up with this worthless nig...I mean, black dude."

"I find that word offensive," Sarah says.

"Yeah, me too. You think I don't hear it? Nobody's quite sure what I am, but I get that thrown at me. The point is this guy is twenty years old, she's fifteen. He doesn't give a shit about her. If I don't look out for her, who will?"

"I thought she was your girlfriend. I'm sorry."

"You thought a whole lot of things that weren't true. I called her a *slut,* because that's what she was acting like. And *that* makes her my girlfriend?"

"Another word, Rafael, that I as a woman find offensive."

"Sensitive, huh? But okay, I get that."

The waitress finally returns with her credit card and receipt. Sarah signs and stands to leave.

"Why you doing this? The lunch, the apologies, and all?" he asks.

"If I tell you, you'll laugh. It'll give you power over me."

"Now that's funny. C'mon, tell me why. You owe me," Rafael says.

"I was told to love every thing and every person I can."

"That's crazy, even for you. And impossible. Hey, am I your first attempt? I'm not too lovable, am I?"

"Easier than I thought. You can't love somebody you know nothing about. I know you a little. I like what I've learned." Sarah pauses, still standing at the table. "Maybe I'm crazy. But maybe you've got to be crazy to love anybody."

"For sure it ain't rational."

"So I've discovered," she adds.

"Why'd you hit me?" An honest question.

"Oh, I don't know. I am very sorry I did it. I got you all wrong. You should file charges. I'm a dangerous woman."

"Man, I've seen way worse than you," Rafael consoles. "Not to dwarf my manhood or anything, but it really hurt. But I knew later, you know, when I was lying in bed and thinking about the whole thing…"

"Knew what?"

"I felt bad for you," he says.

"Really? You felt bad *for me?*"

"Yeah, because I knew you were a minister. My mom brought me to your church a couple times. I can't say I was paying much attention because I was sketching all over the bulletin and day-dreaming. But I knew who you were. And I could tell you were in trouble."

"I was in a lot of trouble," she says as they climb back to the main floor. "I'm still in a lot of trouble. I'm working on it. How old did you say you were? Seventeen?"

"Sixteen."

"Okay, at sixteen, you're supposed to be confused..."

"I'm not really confused," he tells her.

"Okay. But I am. And I'm 69 years old."

Now they're again on 125th Street, and for some reason there's a break in the traffic and it's incredibly quiet at that moment.

"What are you confused about?" he wants to know.

"That's not a simple question."

"Make it simple," Rafael says.

"I'll try. About life, about trust. About God. About death. What it all means."

"My friend Emilio, he died sixteen days ago. He didn't die from drugs or street violence or anything like you'd expect up here. He had asthma. Treatable fucking asthma. And a shitty life. You know, that's what it all meant for him."

"I hope your life turns out like you want it to," Sarah says after an uncomfortable pause, and then she gives him an awkward hug. "I'll pray for you."

"You don't need to," Rafael says, "but thanks?"

‡ ‡ ‡

As she drifts west, so does a gathering dark mass of clouds above her. Sarah's heart and belly are both full and she's caught up in the moment. It is spring. Love is possible, even if delivered in fragments, and must be practiced. She can live in a gray world without absolutes. She can live with doubt, with imperfect faith.

As she patiently waits for a light to change, her phone begins to vibrate pleasurably in her pocket. It must be Darby and this thought pleases her. She doesn't even check the screen information on the incoming call. She answers and it is not Darby.

Like a dog choking on his chain comes the angry yelping voice. "What the hell were you thinking?" The next three words are separated by emphatic pauses: *"I...mean...really?"*

"Who is this?" Sarah briefly holds the phone away from her ear, fearing more screeching is to come.

"I'm curious how you define the word *sermon,"* a quieter but no less agitated voice delivers. "I thought it was an inspirational message to one's congregation, not a session with one's therapist!"

"I thought you were in Boston," she says simply. The light has changed but she does not join the procession of pedestrians who cross the street en masse. She considers hanging up, but simply examines the sky which has been swiftly overtaken by the funereal clouds.

"I could have been trout fishing in Alaska and still would have heard the mass discontent," the voice continues. "The phone at the parsonage has not stopped ringing. Explain!"

Now the wind kicks up and bits of light trash fly loose from the city's waste bins. It looks like late evening and there's a low rumbling emanating from the Bronx.

She's lost for an explanation at the moment, but manages, "My congregation deserves my honesty."

"Then perhaps you'd like to share details of your menstrual cycle. Any weight gain? Problems with constipation or frigidity?"

She marvels at his misinformation and misperceptions. She had once revered him.

"You're out of line, Pastor," she tells the voice in the phone.

"*You* are out of line, Sarah! Your sermon was out of line. I should have read it first. When you gave me the title, I thought of Thomas. But no, no doubting Thomas were you. You entertained your congregation with tales of thinly veiled adultery, obsessive drinking... possibly even homosexual acts."

Here Sarah laughs. "Are we not open and affirming?"

"You are still by law and covenant tied to your husband!" he answers. "And what also upset many of your congregants was this craziness about an apparition. Honestly, an apparition?"

"Wasn't Christ himself an apparition? A post-life presence?" she asks.

A spear of lightning melodramatically flashes across the sky. Then more rumbling from the Bronx.

"Heresy!" he shouts, and then more calmly, as if talking to a teenager who has broken her curfew, "I'm truly worried about you, Sarah. We gave you time to sort things out. Everyone has doubts. I've had doubts. But you are in serious danger, Sarah. I called William. I had to. He said he's free this evening if you'd like to sit down and talk."

Now the clouds open and send forth fat drops of rain like splattering mud. Everyone is diving for cover, but Sarah remains huddled over her phone.

"I suggest you go back to wherever it is that you're living these days and wait for your husband," he instructs.

"It's a big job," Sarah says calmly. "Maybe Bennetta should come with him."

"Bennetta? Yes, of course, if you like. I'll call her."

"No need."

"Go home, Sarah."

"And you can go to hell," she spits out. Then slicing through the thick rain and four lanes of traffic—in a flawless, arching shot—flies her cell phone into a waiting trash bin.

No one takes notice. The sidewalks are nearly empty. Sarah collapses to her knees and all her repressed rage erupts in long, wordless wails. She senses that there is no fairness on this earth, no grace, no mercy, no human understanding.

"What the hell do you want from me?" she hollers at the dark and empty heavens. "Why have you turned your back on me?" But there comes no answer, only the rain and the rush of traffic and sporadic thunder.

Finally she lowers her head, and there before her is an outstretched palm lined with dirty creases. She hears a voice but does not look up.

"For he crushes me with a tempest, and multiplies my wounds without cause; he will not let me get my breath, but fills me with bitterness."

"Job 9," she says.

"You know, Sarah, if you keep screaming at the sky like that, your poor husband is going to be signing papers on your behalf. Especially because you're yelling at someone you're convinced isn't listening."

Now she does look at him, the spiritual nomad. This time his long curls are oily and limp, his face is unshaven, his sparse clothing dirty and tattered. And he is shoeless, of course. Here is a man few would even notice as he passed; they might even be more comfortable looking away.

"Did you think I would abandon you now?" he asks kindly.

"Homeless still?" she asks.

"Seems I need something from you."

"I can't imagine what," she says as she allows him to pull her to her feet, "but help yourself to whatever's left."

"Self-sacrifice and surrender. The perfect Christian."

"I've had enough mockery," Sarah says without bitterness.

"It's not you I'm mocking. Let's walk."

Sarah removes her shoes and leaves them behind. She takes his hand and they continue westward in what has become a light drizzle. The worst has passed. "You've come to take me. I'm dying, aren't I?" she asks.

He stops and exhales a deep, snorting laugh, fragrant with the scent of fried food and something stale and yeasty. "That's rich! What am I? *Psychic?*"

As they walk on, the rain stops completely and the sun appears. They reach a subway station and with a bow and sweep of his arm he announces, "It seems Brooklyn, only Brooklyn, lies in your immediate future."

"To see Darby? Look at me!"

"So you have decided to meet him. I sense forward movement," he says. "Do you have any money? I seem to be missing my wallet."

"I have credit cards, but I'm a little hesitant to use them. I may no longer have a job."

"Oh yes, that. Well, let's just say that here's your first opportunity to exhibit a little faith." He takes her across the street to a vendor with a large, makeshift tent. Brightly colored African dresses and scarves fly in the meek breeze. Leather sandals dangle from the tent supports.

"This isn't really me," she tells him.

"C'mon, be a sport. It goes so well with your name."

‡ ‡ ‡

Back in the subway station, Sarah hands her Metro card to him once she has passed through, but he ducks under without paying. "Just a little venial sin," he whispers. "No eternal damnation for that."

The train is crowded, but Sarah is offered a seat, which, at her age, she finds to be both a blessing and a vague insult. He locks both hands around the bar above her and hangs there like a monkey leering through the bars of his cage. He is uncomfortably close but emotionally distant.

"Tell my father hullo for me," he says almost dismissively.

"Which one?"

"The painter. Your lover," he quips.

Sarah ignores the sexual reference. "Anything else I should tell him?"

"I could ask you to tell him I love him, but I doubt he'd believe you."

The seat next to her is now empty and he sits. Their bodies touch at arm, hip, and leg, and the heat pushes from him in pulsing waves. A slick of sweat covers her face as her entire body warms, as if she has slipped into a hot bath. Two men in suits frown and step away.

"Just tell him thanks for all the things he did right for me," he says quietly. "You know he actually saved my life when I was a little kid, at the beach house."

"I'm confused," she says. "You mean while you were swimming? You disappeared under the water. I thought the sea just threw you back on shore."

"Oh yeah, that's true, but my scrawny little lungs were full of water. I wasn't breathing. Darby pumped my chest and forced air back into my lungs. I coughed. I lived."

Sarah wipes her face with the sleeve of her new dress. Here is the third telling of this story she has endured. *Which version is true? Could they all be?*

"He saved you? Did you always know that?"

"Abraham Darby," he announces. "A hero without a cause."

She stares at his profile, the radiant and filthy face still so aristocratic in the harsh, artificial light. *What has he learned in this life of his, so short, undivinable, and full of longing?* He seems so solid there next to her, and though people around them respond to him, she knows he is not real. He is not of this earth. Neither angel nor demon, but just a man on the subway, in transit.

"What do you want from me?" She leans closer so that her lips are only inches from the hot, hard plane of his cheek. "How can I help you?"

"Connect him," Yago says, still looking ahead expressionlessly. "Connect him to me."

"Is that it?"

"Sadly, I failed at that," he says, and then again, "connect my father to me."

Five simple words. Impossible, if she thinks too hard on it. Possible, if she does not. "Yes, of course," is all she says.

Yago stands and she already feels the weight of his absence. "This is my stop," he says. He bends towards her and kisses her on the mouth, briefly but with great tenderness.

"I never really cared for Brooklyn," he tells her flippantly as the subway doors close between their two worlds.

‡ ‡ ‡

Sarah leans against one of the legendary London Planes that ring the park. Across the street, Darby is still at his table, working his way through the Sunday *Times*. Angelo remains by his side with his nose buried in a comic book.

She has been given something, she realizes as she watches them, hiding in the noise and commotion in the park behind her. For as much as she has lost, she no longer feels abandoned. For as elusive as faith may be, perhaps it is always present. Faith like that of Johnny, or especially Angelo, both burned by loss, but defiantly pretending normalcy. Their ridiculous and irrational faith that mercy and grace will rebound has been weakened but remains ever present.

She replays in her mind Darby's seductions and Alexander's admonition to love her way back to God. She recalls the dares of Alejandra. Thinks of Yago's erotic pleading and reassuring presence. She had been disconnected, difficult to reach. Something has jarred free and it is enough to keep her sane.

Sarah takes the long walk across Court Street to Darby. He looks up, cocks his head at her flamboyant dress and muddy, sandaled feet. Angelo just grins and returns to his comic.

"What section would you like?" Darby asks, pushing the messy stack towards her.

"Arts and Leisure. Maybe I'll read something about you."

"There is a wee bit on page 12. Really ridiculous," he says. "Listen, Sarah, we have to talk."

"Yes, Darby," she answers. "We will talk. After dinner. My place."

CHAPTER TWENTY • CERULEAN BLUE FOREVER

An Evening Some Time Later

AFTER THE DINNER DISHES HAVE BEEN CLEARED AWAY, Angelo and Johnny sit at the kitchen table and stare at the letter placed between them. The envelope is a crisp parchment, all golden and splotchy like the top of a pie. It is inscribed in Alejandra's flowing penmanship with Angelo's name and address.

"Shall I read it to you? I know script is weird for you," Johnny says.

"Okay, but read slow. I'll close my eyes so I can see her talking to me."

There are no windows in the floor-through's kitchen, but the low lighting suggests a sinking sun. Johnny hands the letter to his son. "Here. You should open it."

Angelo sticks his pudgy index finger in a small gap at the top of the flap. "I don't want to rip it."

Johnny brings him a butter knife and together they make a clean cut across the top.

"I want to save the stamps, too," Angelo says. "Go ahead, Daddy. Read it."

And so Johnny begins:

To My Sweetness, Angelo,

As I flew back to my home, I brought with me much sadness. As our plane parted the clouds and touched the perfect blue sky, I thought of my son. I wondered where did that beautiful, joyful spirit go? Where lives the soul that had no boundaries? I miss him more every day and this I know I share with you, dearest Angelo.

These are things that I do not understand. How can I explain them to you? I think maybe in writing this to you, we might understand them together just a little better.

Your Papa was filled with love for you. I saw this and I know it because it is how I loved him. A parent's love is like a bucket always full. Even when water washes out, it is at once refilled. So you must know that even though you do not see him every day, he is with you, this love that death cannot take from you. You may talk to him, share all your worries and happinesses, and Yago will hear you. Of this I am sure.

As for me and you, mi nieto, we are as one, in family. In the summer months I will bring you to Escazú, if Johnny can bear to let you go for an entire month, maybe even two! There the gentle waters of the sea will hold you in her arms as she held your Papa long ago. There together we will work to heal our hearts.

I will also add a little meat to your bones, which you need, and never cut your hair!

Until then, you must send me messages with your heart and prayers.

Tu Abuelita

Johnny folds the letter and returns it to the envelope. "Keep this in a safe place, son. We may need to read it again."

"I already talk to Papa and he talks to me," the boy says.

"Then you may need to help your grandmother with that when you see her."

"Can I go, like she said?"

"After school is out, I will decide. It costs quite a bit to fly that far from Brooklyn."

"Darby and me talked about…"

"Darby and I," his father corrects.

"You talked about it, too?"

Johnny taps his palm on his forehead. "Just go on with your story."

"Darby told me about where Abuelita lives when we ate lunch. He said it was like a place in your dreams, real pretty like it wasn't real. He went there a lot of times. Maybe I can go with him?"

Now there's a thought to keep Johnny up at night. "We'll see," his father dodges. "Bedtime is our first mission."

Hours later, Johnny is sitting alone in their living room with all the lights off, but a dozen different candles are burning all around the room. The cookie jar has been placed on the coffee table next to a nearly finished bottle of red wine.

In his hands is a disc, a compilation of music he burned for Yago, his greatest hits. There's Motown, disco, torch songs, and ballads. He has not yet, but would like to play the eleventh song. Their song without it ever being called that. The traffic on Court Street and the knowledge that his son sleeps in another room are his sole reassurances that life continues. It now seems frightening and unpredictable. This world without his husband seems colorless. No depth, no vibrancy. For all the grief that man caused him, the simple joy Yago brought to everyday life—on his good days, which were most days—was a gift he will not receive again.

When Alejandra came to help sort through Yago's things, they had decided instead to take Angelo to a matinee. All his clothes, his music, his scents and many toiletries, his favorite mug, and all the things hidden in drawers that only Yago opened, all these went untouched. Before leaving, Alejandra had asked only for a shirt that had her son's scent buried in the fabric. All else she required, she had said, was locked safely in her heart.

Then he remembers how Yago would shake away worries and concerns, even mild depressions. Dance. All these calamities inhabit the mind. In dancing, in being only in the wonderful world of muscle and movement, of rhythm and raucous disengagement, Yago could return to happiness. And in the arms of a person he loved—like any one of the people who shared this space—dance became a real and tangible expression of that love.

So Johnny, half drunk and in tears, walks slowly to their black, oversized, outdated audio system. He removes the Martha Reeves disc that was, he supposes, the last one Yago danced to. Johnny's fingers are now where Yago's were, and Johnny places the disc back into its plastic case with great reverence. He lays the new one onto the circular bed, closes the tray, advances to the eleventh track. Hits pause.

He knows the version of the song that will play, Yago's favorite version, although he has recordings of four. It is not the booming, swinging Sinatra rendition that was his least favorite. Not the crazy, disjointed Cher version in which the upbeat, Middle Eastern–style music clashes with the slowly delivered lyrics. And Liza Minnelli, of course, comes in a close second with her pared down, melodramatic delivery. Liza, however, did change the lyrics ever so slightly, a serious transgression in Yago's appraisal.

It is Connie Francis who takes the cake. Her voice is sweet, tragically romantic, and pleasantly syrupy like the lyrics themselves. And the big, bold finish, cymbals and all, cannot be surpassed.

Johnny hits play and is stunned by the new beauty he hears in the brief piano and percussion introduction. Then, full and unadorned, comes Connie's voice.

If it takes forever I will wait for you
For a thousand summers I will wait for you

He closes his eyes and raises both arms and places his hands on the shoulders he is imagining. Following a lead that is not his, he takes the wide—too wide for him—strides locked into the rhythm of both music and lyric. He sings along.

Anywhere you wander, anywhere you go
Every day remember how I love you so

Now they dance flawlessly, Ginger and Fred, around the small living room, laughing, throwing off waves of body heat. They dance on, not tripping over the hassock, not knocking over either wine bottle or cookie jar. It is like movie dancing, flawless and angelic. Their feet barely touch the floor, making no sound that might disturb their neighbors below.

In your heart believe what in my heart I know
That forevermore I'll wait for you

Then right at the very end, at the emotional, vocal, and orchestral crescendo, just before that moment when Yago would have dipped Johnny back so low that they would sometimes fall together to the floor, right then a yawning Angelo, rubbing his eyes, stands in the wide entrance to the room.

The music ends and Johnny hurries to shut off the player.

Angelo is motionless and quiet for a moment, squinting into the candlelit room. Then, with his penguin clutched to his chest, he walks over and tucks into the corner of the couch.

"You told me Papa wasn't here anymore."

Johnny can't speak. His son is swallowed up by the old couch, so small and helpless he seems. But what eyes he has, to have witnessed his spinner of tales of fantasy now make his own fantastical appearance.

"Shall I play the song again?" Johnny manages to ask. "Would you like that?"

"Dance one more time." Angelo brings his knees up and wraps his two arms, like the flexible twigs of a young tree, around his tiny trunk. Then with unwavering concentration, the boy watches as the two people he loves most in the world say goodbye to each other.

EPILOGUE

DARBY WAS RIGHT. THE MANNING GALLERY LOVED HIS NEW work but changed the title from "Grief: A Retrospective" to "Abraham Darby: Absence." He had been joking when he gave them the original title for his tight, venal collection; they had missed that. "Absence," the board members explained, was both elegiac and yet more open to interpretation than "Grief." Mere grief would have been a hard sell.

Amazingly, most of the critics bought it, and wrote what Darby deemed to be "a lot of wordy, self-important bullshit." There were assertions about how, one revered reviewer wrote, "through masterful and beautifully detailed depictions of trivial objects, Darby has created in the mind of the viewer the converse image of what is truly meaningful." Another proclaimed that "given the pared-down, domestic nature of many of the subjects, Darby evokes the deep significance and value of family and everyday life."

The exhibit's curator, peevish and uncomfortable when she had been confronted with Darby's self-portrait in the bathroom mirror, had deemed it "a little too dark" and better included in a "future show." And that was fine with him.

What they were never shown was the final painting of Yago, wings, ashes, and all. That painting was a gift by the artist to a small restaurant in Brooklyn, where it received rave reviews—and more deservedly so—by owner, family, and clientele. There the portrait will remain for years to come, uninsured and in less-than-ideal conditions for conservation, but in the perfect position to protect what mattered most to the subject.

ACKNOWLEDGEMENTS

There are many people who were instrumental in the development of the themes, content, and appearance of this book. I would like to thank:

Martin and Judith Shepard for their confidence in me and in the survival of literary fiction of all sorts. No writer could have better publishers or friends;

Joslyn Pine for her meticulous and thoughtful editing (and for donating a piece of her soul in the process), and Lon Kirschner for his intriguing cover design;

Reverend Dianne Rodriguez of the drifters' church, First Parish, in Northville, New York for her initial discontent with the portrayal of Sarah Obadias. She encouraged me to dig deeper into Sarah's psyche and her marital, sexual, and faith crises;

Susan Roecker for her patient inspiration and art direction;

Barbara Zegarek, Linda Murphy, and Anne E. Trimble—cheerleaders, supporters, and my unflappable friends;

Meryl Zegarek, my brilliant can-do publicist;

The entire Kilts family for the world of gifts they bestow upon me on a daily basis, as well as my mother and father, who taught us how to be loving and generous and, on our best days, really funny.

A NOTE ON THE TYPOGRAPHY

The text font in this novel, Adobe Garamond, is named after the simple abode in New Mexico where Manuel "the Man" Garamond created this typeface. Manuel was a gay and flamboyant doodler which is evident in the playful yet mannered serifs of this now classic font.

Seriously, few people care a stitch about typestyles or take the time to read about them at a novel's end. I do, however, love typography and chose Adobe Garamond for the font's elegance and readability.

Other characters in the type cast are the pompous Felix Titling, the wine-loving Gill Sans, and the understated and oft humorous Nicolas Cochin. There is great art in them all and I thank them for their participation in *Paint the Bird*.